A STONE
FOR THE
JOURNEY

A STONE
FOR THE
JOURNEY

ROCHELLE
WISOFF-FIELDS

OPEN ROAD

INTEGRATED MEDIA

NEW YORK

Copyright © 2018 by Rochelle Wisoff-Fields

ISBN: 978-1-5040-7769-9

This edition published in 2022 by Open Road Integrated Media, Inc.
180 Maiden Lane
New York, NY 10038
www.openroadmedia.com

To Lois Spears,
At a time when I felt awkward and out of place, you stepped in and
encouraged me to spread my creative wings.
This book is your legacy.

A STONE
FOR THE
JOURNEY

THE JOURNEY BEGINS

1889 -1903

IN HER FATHER'S FOOTSTEPS

The *Heder* teacher's face turned crimson. He narrowed his eyes and glared at five-year-old Havah as if she were a piglet about to be dumped on his doorstep. Then he clenched his tobacco-stained teeth and spat a brown glob on the doorstep.

Up until this moment, she had been excited to learn to read the Torah, the words that came from Adoshem's own mouth. Huddled against Papa's shoulder, she hid her eyes in his coat folds.

"You can't be serious, Rabbi Shimon. She's a girl."

"So, she is." Papa's arm tightened around her. "My daughter's mind is every whit as keen as her brother Mendel's."

"To be certain she's a bright one, and one day she'll be a most excellent wife and mother. Perhaps she'll even marry a rabbi herself, but, Rebbe, to come to *Heder* with boys? It's not right."

"Where does the Torah say it's wrong for a girl to learn?"

"Rabbi Ben Hyrcanus clearly stated in the Talmud that to teach a daughter Torah is *tiflut*—obscenity. And did he not also say that the words of the Torah should be burned rather than be entrusted to a woman? Rabbi, you of all people should know this."

"As far as I'm concerned, it's opinion and rubbish! Didn't the prophet Yo'el write 'your sons *and* daughters shall prophecy?' Miriam and Devorah, were they not judges in Israel?"

"You win, Rebbe."

"I always do."

A STONE FOR THE JOURNEY

The rabbi shut his prayer book. "May HaShem grant us strength to see beyond our sorrow and may the name of Edith Cohen be blessed."

Eight-year-old Havah Cohen gazed at the newly unveiled headstone. *Could my sweet grandmother who taught me to knead* Hollah *dough and sing blessings really be buried under the grass? Isn't it hot and dark?*

Mama placed a large pebble on the marker.

Havah tugged at Mama's sleeve. "Why do we put rocks on graves when Christians put flowers on them?"

Kneeling, Mama wrapped her arm around Havah's shoulders. "What happens after you pick a flower?"

"It turns brown and dies."

"Can a rock die?"

"Uh-uh."

"A stone is eternal, like your grandmother's soul. The more stones you see on a person's grave, the more he or she has been remembered."

Havah opened her clenched fist and dropped a handful of pebbles. "I will never forget you, Bubbe."

CAST FROM HER FATHER'S HOUSE

Gunshots and screaming woke sixteen-year-old Havah Cohen from a sound and dreamless sleep. She ran to her window. Flames shot through the roof of the synagogue. Dense clouds of black smoke poured through the windows as men with shovels and rocks smashed the stained glass. By moonlight, she could see her older brother lying beside the road in a bloodstained night shirt. Her other brother, a few feet away, lay face down.

"Papa!" she screamed when she saw him run from the inferno clutching the sacred scrolls. Before she could utter another word, her bedroom door crashed open. A strange man grabbed her around the waist and a rough hand covered her mouth. She struggled to free herself. He pushed her down on the bed, his body pressing against hers. Paralyzed with fear and repulsed by the odor of liquor, she choked and gasped for breath.

Out of the corner of her eye, she saw her mother creep through the doorway and inch toward the bed with a wooden rolling pin high over her head. She slammed it down on the back of the man's head. With a sudden jerk and a grunt, he released Havah, rolled off her, and fell to the floor unconscious.

She sat up, clutching a pillow, and stared down at him. Blood pooled under his head and seeped into the cracks between the floor boards. *This has to be a dream. In the morning, Papa will wink at her over breakfast and assure her it had all been a horrendous nightmare.*

Her mother yanked her hand, dragged her from the bed, and held her for a moment; her tears hot on Havah's neck.

Taking Havah's face between her hands, Mama kissed her forehead. "Hurry, Havah. May the God of Israel go with you."

"But Mama—"

Seizing Havah's arm, her mother dragged her to the back door of the house and shoved her out. "No arguing! Go! Whatever you do, don't look back!"

Heart thumping, Havah ran. Thick smoke stung her eyes and burned her throat. Ignoring Mama's charge, she stopped and turned. The blazing synagogue crumbled to the ground.

ORPHANED

"Run, Havah!" The sound of her mother's last scream filled Havah's head and pounded in rhythm to her footsteps.

Beech trees loomed in the forest ahead; their gnarled roots circled above the ground like dancers at a wedding feast. They whispered somber melodies.

Rocks, frozen grass, and thorns stabbed the soles of her bare feet. There had been no time for shoes, no time to dress.

Who will pray for their souls? Who will remember David, the artist, or Mendel, the poet, or Mama or Papa?

She compelled her heavy mouth to shape the Hebrew prayer—Kaddish—prayer for the dead and prayer for the bereft. *"Magnified and sanctified is Your great name . . ."* She detested its beauty.

Her hands, held her over her ears, could not blot out the cries of friends and neighbors, fast becoming memories. *". . . in the world, which you have created . . ."*

Thorns grabbed at her nightgown and she fought to ignore the fire in her lungs. *". . . according to Your will."*

Run!

Brambles ripped into her flesh.

Run!

The muscles of her legs burned.

Don't stop! Run!

Havah shivered as the wind whipped around and through her. But stronger than the cold was her determination. When she could no longer run, she walked, the heat of the flames scorching her back.

Her tongue stuck to her frozen lips. *"Let His great name be blessed forever and to all eternity."*

RABBI SHIMON COHEN

Five-year-old Havah flexed her stinging hand. "Why did the Almighty make honey bees?"

Shimon Cohen's onyx eyes glistened and his beard tickled her nose. "So we don't forget."

"Forget what?"

"The good things in life are made sweeter by affliction."

He was her teacher, her father, her world.

By the time she turned sixteen, he proclaimed her a scholar equal to any of his *Yeshiva* students. "Someday, maybe not in my lifetime, Havah, women will read Torah in the shul and not have to hide from the narrow minds of men. Perhaps your daughter will be the first woman to become a rabbi."

His voice, low and soothing, still rumbled like distant thunder in her mind.

How could he be dead? It seemed only last night that he had tucked her in as he had every night since she was a child.

She had nodded off reading. He slipped the book from her hands and kissed her forehead.

Filled with a sudden sense of dread, she threw her arms around his neck. "I love you so much it hurts, Papa!"

"What's wrong, Havaleh?"

"What if I never have another chance to tell you? It would sorrow all my days!"

He chuckled and snuffed the lamp on her bed table. "Sleep now so that splendid head of yours will be sharp in the morning."

Hours later, Cossacks shot him down, clutching the sacred Torah scrolls before the flaming synagogue.

Rain pelted the window over her new bed. "I'm a stranger in a strange land." Scooching under the covers, she buried her head in the down pillow. *Will life ever be sweet again?* "I love you so much it hurts, Papa."

The wind whispered, "I know."

MIRIAM COHEN

While Papa was the High Priest of their home, Miriam Cohen was the *balabusteh,* the homemaker. There was no doubt in Havah's mind that he would have been helpless without her. Havah lost count of the times he had misplaced something and grew frantic searching for it. In her calm, gentle way, Mama never failed to find the missing article.

Papa would draw her to his chest and recite in a resonant voice. "'Who can find an *eshet khayeel,* a woman of virtue and strength? She's worth more than rubies.'"

As a child, Havah looked forward to her mother's flaky fried pastries loaded with raisins and crispy potato latkes. Even though Hanukkah only lasted eight days, Mama started cooking her special treats several days before. She loved celebrations and said a mere week was not long enough.

The year Havah turned sixteen, Mama brought home potatoes from the market a month before Hanukkah. Havah, who hated grating them, groaned, "We've never started this early."

"Why wait, Havaleh?" Mama cupped her hand around Havah's cheek and pinched her chin. "Who knows? This may be the last time we celebrate."

There was an urgent plea in the way Mama said "last time" that chilled Havah as she grated potatoes for her new family two months later. Sometimes Mama dreamed things that came true. *Did she hear the gunshots, shattering glass, and screams in her sleep? Did she know Natalya, their peaceful village, would go up in flames and smoke in less than two weeks?*

SVECHKA

To call the backward village Svechka 'the candle' seemed a contradiction to Arel Gitterman. Perhaps, at the time of its founding, the Russians considered it a place of enlightenment. However, in the present, shacks and rundown shops lined the dirt roads.

A few Christians remained in the town, but Jewish peasants made up the majority of the population. This suited Arel for he had no love for the *goyim*.

He approached the largest building in Svechka—the core of the Jewish community, the synagogue or shul, the linchpin that held them together. When he opened the door, the scent of musty books and the aroma of linseed oil greeted him like old friends. The solid oak woodwork was polished to a warm sheen. Elaborate carvings of plants, birds, and animals, including a half-lion, adorned the Holy Ark, an ornate cabinet containing the sacred scrolls. It sat behind the bema, the central platform. Four columns and railings surrounded it.

The balcony where the women observed the Sabbath made a circle close to the canopy of the high ceiling. A stairway led to the door on the west side of the sanctuary. Sun streamed through the high windows and bathed the women's gallery.

Tables had been arranged side by side, like stalwart soldiers, around the *bemah*. They stood ready for the men to study, to discuss and argue points of law. Arel took his place at one of them and opened his *Humash*. Reading the familiar words that were life and light to his people, he grinned. "Svechka, the perfect name for this place after all."

HAVAH COHEN

No matter how hard Arel Gitterman tried to focus his attention on the page in front of him, the words only taunted him. For as much as he tried to concentrate on his studies, the letters might as well have walked off the paper.

Since the Shabbos morning they found her, half-dressed and bleeding on the steps of the synagogue, he had thought of little else. *Where had she come from? How is it that she sang the mourner's Kaddish in her sleep as I carried her to the Levine's home? Who would have taught the sacred words to a girl?*

"A shame," Hershel's voice broke into Arel's reverie, "my wife had no choice but to chop off half of her foot. If she hadn't, the child would surely have died. But who will want to take a cripple as his bride? Our poor little Havah." Curling smoke from his pipe floated to the ceiling. "Nonetheless, she is a beauty."

"Havah." Her name became the melody Arel canted with his daily prayers. "Havah." *Could there be a sweeter name under heaven?* Havah, it meant life. The name of the first woman on earth. "Havah." He could not stop repeating it.

Her face occupied his every daytime thought. What if she was a demon child, as his brother-in-law claimed after all, and had bewitched him? Her eyes that he had seen ever so briefly haunted him. He saw them at night as he drifted off to sleep, dark and almost too large for her face. She leaped through his dreams, her long gown and wavy black hair fluttering behind her. When he awoke to the cold light of dawn, his mind repeated the cycle.

FRUMA YA'EL LEVINE

A multitude of sparkling windows, all framed by colorful curtains, bore witness to Fruma Ya'el's love of light. "There's enough darkness in this world," she said, "but not in my home."

Above all else, Havah had learned Fruma Ya'el valued cleanliness. Woe to the poor unfortunate who dared to track mud across her wooden floors. A hungry mouse would be hard-pressed to find so much as a cracker crumb under her table. A gnat would starve to death in this house.

Afternoon sunlight bathed the generous kitchen with a comfortable glow. On the stove a kettle of chicken soup bubbled. Its savory aroma helped lessen Havah's loneliness for her family. The baby boy on Fruma Ya'el's lap cooed as she fastened his diaper. Havah fought the urge to pinch his pudgy thigh.

"Such a sweet little mensch. I'll give you some ointment for his rash," said Auntie Fruma. "As for his colic, don't eat so many onions."

The child's mother hovered over her shoulder. "Onions? But I love them."

"Love them less until he's weaned. Remember, what you eat," Fruma Ya'el bundled him in his blanket and gave him back to her, "he eats."

Holding the infant against her breast, the young mother bent to kiss Fruma Ya'el's cheek. "Thank you, Auntie. There's a new hen in your chicken pen for your troubles."

"Troubles? *Feh!* My joy. My pleasure." Fruma Ya'el's dark eyes shone. "*Azay Gezundt*, be healthy. That is my payment."

As the girl left, Havah shifted her gaze to her adopted aunt. "Did you deliver him?"

"My daughter, there's not a child born in Svechka I haven't brought into the world."

THE COHEN BROTHERS

Not a day went by that Havah did not think about her family taken from her too soon. In the night, they came alive in her dreams. During the day, they were never far from her thoughts.

"I see those tears," said Fruma Ya'el as she mashed potatoes. "Speak to me, my daughter."

"Mendel had the most intense brown eyes." Havah popped a raisin into her mouth. She squeezed it between her teeth. The sweetness exploded on her tongue. "He was eight years older than I and studying to be a rabbi like Papa.

"When I turned twelve, Papa said the boys in my *Heder* class would never learn Holy writ with such a comely distraction." Havah's cheeks blazed. "So, he decided Mendel should become my tutor. Such a teacher, he was strict but kind."

"What was your other brother like?" asked Fruma Ya'el.

"He never cared much for studying Torah or Midrash. 'What *dybbik* left this dizzy *vontz* on our doorstep?' Papa would say. 'I asked the Almighty for scholars, not artists.' But truly, he was proud of David's gift. Once, David did a painting of daffodils for Mama. They looked so real, I could almost smell them."

With a suppressed sigh, she covered the braided loaves with clean towels and set them on the back of the stove to rise. "The last *Shabbos* with my family, I baked *Hollah*. I couldn't put raisins in it because David ate all of them. I can still see him with Mama's clean dish towel over his head, walking bent over. He sang all raspy like an old lady, too. 'Little Bubbe Fuss Bucket. All astir over a raisin. A raisin. A shriveled little raisin. *Oy, yoy, yoy.*'"

"I wish I hadn't gotten so mad. I said horrid things."

Fruma Ya'el unfolded a linen tablecloth. She snapped it so it billowed and dropped to cover the table. "Were they the last words you spoke to him?"

"No." Havah stirred the kettle of chicken soup on the stove and breathed in the aroma. "I could never stay mad at him. If only I'd known—"

"Would you have done anything differently?"

"No."

Crafted to look like a tree in the wind, the main stem of the candelabra curved with nine branches arching in opposite directions. The candle cups sat upon them like majestic crowns. Between seven of the branches and the trunk, an opening hosted a pair of doves, positioned breast to breast, perched on a flower-covered vine, spreading their graceful wings. The vine twined around the trunk, ending at the wide base.

"Arel, tell Havah about my papa's masterpiece," said Yussel.

Proud of its history, on most occasions, Arel was usually more than willing to recount the story. Tonight, captivated by her eyes, sparkling like black diamonds, speech eluded him. *Did Adam feel this way in the Garden of Eden when he brought the succulent fruit to his hungry lips?* "My grandfather, of blessed memory, was a rabbi, as was his father before him, and an artist. After my grandmother died, he made this menorah in her memory. She was very young."

"What did she die of?" asked Havah, innocently.

"Christian poison! Tell her, Arel!" Yussel's bony hands curled into fists. "Cossacks shot her down before my eyes fifty-three years ago. Like yesterday, I remember."

"You must've been a boy."

"Five years old. Her *Yosi,* her heart, she called me."

A tear rolled down Havah's pale cheek. "You can tell how much he loved her by the verse he chose to engrave on the menorah, '*Behold, you are lovely. Your eyes are like doves.*'"

Under his breath, Arel whispered, "Yes, they are."

AREL GITTERMAN

Halfway through a night of tossing and turning, Havah rammed her fist into her pillow. *It's wrong. He's betrothed to another. No, not just another, my sister!*

Adopted sister, her inner self argued.

Arel's image had haunted her since their introduction. His hair and beard and ink shadows framed a face as pale as dawn.

It's an arranged marriage. She swaddled her head with the down pillow. *He only agreed to it because he didn't know me.*

His voice, deep and gentle, belonged to a studious man, the kind of man Havah, a rabbi's daughter, dreamed of—Rabbi Yussel's only son.

Arel, a strong name. Lion of God.

Sleep eluded her as her internal wrestling match continued.

Gittel's tender and sweet. She would never challenge him with Talmud and Torah like I would. What man wouldn't want her? I see the way he looks at her.

Like silver-gray clouds, his prolific eyes spoke silent words directly to her heart.

And what about the way he looks at me?

RABBI YUSSEL
GITTERMAN

Rabbi Gitterman and Havah's adopted family, the Levines, were friends. She looked forward to his frequent visits for he was not put off by her knowledge of the Torah as some men, and always made time to discuss it with her.

One summer evening after supper, while the Levines and the Gittermans chatted over a final glass of wine, Havah excused herself. She sank onto a bench outside the kitchen door and imagined the happy voices inside belonged to her father, mother, and brothers. *Where's the justice in my escape from death without them? Where's the Almighty's mercy Papa used to speak of?*

Absorbed in her lonesome reverie, she did not hear the rabbi's cane scraping the ground, and jumped when he said, "Lovely night to think of your parents, of blessed memory."

"How can you tell? Are you a mind reader?"

He eased himself down beside her. "I'm a good listener."

"When did you . . . lose your eyesight, Rabbi?"

"Fifteen years ago. The fever of 1885 took my bride as well."

"And you still continued to serve as rabbi? Wasn't it difficult? Not being able to read, I mean. Do you ever feel sorry for yourself because you're . . . you're. . . ?"

"Blind? At first, I did. Such blackness. I couldn't breathe. Alone. Trapped. I prayed for death. I pleaded. I begged."

"What changed?"

"I realized the Almighty had shown me His infinite mercy."

Havah bristled. "How can you call losing your wife and your sight His mercy?"

Yussel inclined his head and smiled. "He never promised us happiness, but He has granted us life. And that, my daughter, is Adoshem's mercy."

TOVA GITTERMAN RESNICK

Tova's reflection stared at her from the dusty mirror above her dresser. Her bruised cheeks were sunken and her arms looked like sparse winter branches. Her white teeth had turned gray. The back ones had crumbled and fallen out altogether. Fruma Ya'el called it malnutrition. She constantly scolded her for not drinking enough milk and urged her to eat more meat. Tova turned a deaf ear to her. Her worthless husband drank most of his meager income. *How could I possibly take what little food he provides from our five children's mouths?*

She slipped off her kerchief. Her dull, short curls clung to her head. *What happened to the vivacious girl with raven waves, Rabbi Yussel's eldest daughter, whose hand was sought after by many an eligible scholar?*

At thirty-one, she looked closer to fifty. Years of Feivel's beatings and deprivation had reduced her to an old crone.

How often he hollered it as his whip slashed her shoulders, *"Kronah!"*

"He's turned me into one," she whispered to her weary image.

It did no good to moon over lost beauty. There was only the matter at hand. She turned away from the mirror and lifted her howling newborn from the washtub. Sinking into the rocking chair, still sore from childbirth, she raised the baby to her breast.

As her milk let down, it brought on a pleasant drowsiness. The child's suckling noises soothed her. She imagined this little one as a beautiful young woman.

"I won't live to see it," she murmured. "Bayla, my blessing, you are my final reward."

FEIVEL RESNICK

Feivel slammed the door behind him. He had had his fill of Tova and her self-righteous family. The last thing he wanted was to celebrate another girl with them.

Did I ask for another mouth to feed? For all he knew, she was not even his. She did not resemble him in the slightest. The other four children had his red hair, but not this little dark-haired bastard. She looked only like her ugly mother.

Maybe the old hag had a tryst? His hollow laughter echoed in his own ears. *Ha! Who would have her? All she does is nag. 'Feivel, the window's broken.' 'Feivel, the children need shoes.' 'Feivel this and Feivel that.'*

A light snow began to fall, stinging his eyes and fogging his eyeglasses. He took them off and wiped them on his shirt. Moonlight shining through the clouds accused him.

The crime he'd denied for seventeen years crashed in on him. At fourteen, Tova Gitterman was a beauty. Her gray eyes sparkled like quartz. Tall and supple as a willow, her black hair shone almost blue in the sun. How could a sixteen-year-old man resist her?

He pled for her hand, but her father, the rabbi, betrothed her to another. Feivel went insane with rage. Her image plagued him. Night after night, he dreamed of nothing else.

One afternoon, by the river, he seized his opportunity. He wooed her from her laundry into the woods. Her begging to be set free only fueled his frenzy.

When she was found to be with child, his child, the marriage was quickly arranged. With the desperation of a small animal whose leg is caught in a trap's iron teeth, he drank himself into a stupor on their wedding night and beat her senseless.

Filled with self-loathing, he fell prostrate on the frozen ground, keening, "I'm the monster. Adoshem, forgive me! I don't deserve to live."

ITZAK ABROMOVICH

Havah enjoyed *Shabbes* dinners with the Abromoviches, if for no other reason than the generous portions of laughter they served. Especially Itzak. If not regaling everyone with his stories, often tallish tales, he could melt the coldest heart with his fiddle.

"So, the Professor says to the Cossack, 'Itzak Abromovich from Svechka is the best cabinet maker in all of Moldavia. I'll vouch for him.' Before you can say, 'Adoshem lives,' my travel permission papers are signed and I have more Christian customers than I know what to do with."

To punctuate his words, the stout carpenter waved his short arms and his hand caught his goblet. Havah held her breath as red wine splattered the white linen tablecloth. She looked from the glass to Itzak's wife Shayndel who merely shrugged and blotted the puddle with her napkin.

"Forgive me, my love." Itzak righted his cup. "I'm a clumsy oaf who forgets his manners."

Shaking her head, Shayndel winked at Havah as she poured more wine for him. "A stained tablecloth is a small price to pay for happiness."

SHAYNDEL ABROMOVICH

The more Havah learned about Arel's sister, the more she liked her. In the few months since she had met Shayndel, the bond between them had grown strong.

After her older sister, Sarah, left Svechka for America, Shayndel took on the responsibility of caring for her blind father, Rabbi Yussel, and her brother. On top of keeping the household running smoothly, she helped her sister Tova look after five children with aplomb and good humor.

Shayndel had never been seriously ill. Havah, who caught colds and tired easily, felt weak and pale next to her. Even after an arduous labor with twins, Shayndel's cheeks bloomed with health and vitality.

One of her long braids tumbled from under her nightcap to her waist. It shone golden in the morning light. She quickly tucked it back under the cap to hide her secret.

"I'm glad Itzak didn't let you cut it. Making a woman chop off her hair when she marries is a ridiculous custom." Havah held ten-day-old Mendel against her shoulder and brushed her lips over his silky cheek. "What will you be when you grow up?"

"Perhaps, he'll be a fiddler, like his papa," said Shayndel, holding David to her breast, a sleepy smile spreading her lips. "Both of them will probably be cabinet makers like Itzak and his papa before him."

Havah's chest buzzed with anger and she hissed through gritted teeth. "What if they don't want to be carpenters? What if they hate music? Will you shave their heads and sell them into slavery? Of course not! They're boys. Men!"

Shayndel's smile faded. "Havah's what's vexing you so?"

"Do you know Tova is selling her daughter to the shoemaker, a man nearly twice her age?"

"She's not selling her. It's a fair arrangement. He's a good man, Havah. A gentle man." Shayndel's eyes shone like the sky in summer. "The *shadkhan* arranged my marriage. Look how well it's turned out. There's not a better husband or father in all of Moldavia than my Itzak."

HERSHEL LEVINE

A thin stream of smoke slipped through Uncle Hershel's lips. Havah choked and sneezed. He set his pipe aside. "Forgive me, Havaleh. I see my pipe doesn't agree with my new daughter. Your sister, Gittel, is not so crazy about it either." Stroking his beard, he opened a book and set it front of Havah. "*Nu?* She tells me you read the Holy Language." His bushy eyebrows knit into one. "Is this true?"

Havah trembled. *What will he do if I tell the truth?* The possible forms of punishment flashed through her mind. None of them frightened her as much as the prospect of being denied access to the written word, her solace. She returned his piercing glare. "Yes!"

He pointed to the middle of a page. "Read it to me."

Biting her lower lip, she took a deep breath. "*Betakh el Adoshem b'khol Leebekha . . .*"

"Trust in Adoshem with all your heart," he repeated.

"Shall I continue?"

"No, I've heard enough." His green eyes brimmed, a sharp contrast to his bone-white hair. "Your father, the rabbi, taught you?"

She nodded.

His stern expression softened. "Well then. Who am I to deny the heart of a rabbi's daughter?"

"I may read?"

"Anything you wish. My library is yours."

She seized his hand and covered it with kisses. "Thank you, Uncle!"

"You've been with us these many months. We're *Mishpokhah*—family." He pressed her palm against his cheek. "Will I never be Papa to you?"

GITTEL LEVINE

"Gittel," said Havah, "remember the time you knotted my stockings around the bedpost?"

"It took you an hour to untie them. And you retaliated by hiding my bloomers in the chicken coup." Gittel giggled, combed her hair, and sighed. "Soon, this will be a sweet memory."

Havah wanted nothing more than to hate her adopted sister, but that could never happen. Was it Gittel's fault she was betrothed to the man Havah loved? After all, Gittel and Arel were only children when their fathers signed away their futures.

"Don't let them lop it off." Havah twined a strawberry curl around her finger and kissed Gittel's freckled cheek. "I'll bet Arel would prefer your beautiful tresses left long."

"But it's the law."

Meek as a dove, innocent as a lamb, Gittel embodied the meaning of her name: good, a saint above saints. Uncle Hershel called her his 'flittering magpie'. Havah fought the sudden impulse to embrace her and slap her at the same time. "Show me in the Torah where it says women are to shave their heads to please men."

Setting her comb aside, Gittel threw her arms around Havah's neck, her breath tickling Havah's ear. "Run away with him tonight. I won't say a word. Anyone can see Arel's heart belongs to you."

"Arel does love you, you know."

"Of course, he does, like a sister."

GENESIS

THE FIRST GITTEL LEVINE

Gittel held up her new blouse. "How did I do, Mama?"

Fruma Ya'el inspected the seams. "Your Aunt Gittel, of blessed memory, couldn't have done any better. You've inherited her talent."

Gittel folded the blouse and set it in her lap. "You're a talented seamstress, too, Mama."

"Not like my beautiful sister."

"Do I look like her?"

Gittel's green eyes shone and her thick auburn hair fell over her shoulders in glossy waves. Fruma Ya'el shook her head. "You look like your papa, but no less beautiful, my daughter."

"What was she like? You've never told me anything about her."

"You're seventeen. I suppose you have a right to know about the saint you were named after. She was ten years older than I. After our mother died, Gittel did her best to take Mama's place. When she married your papa, he moved into our house. What a wonderful brother he was! Affectionate. Funny. After six years, they still had no children, but he claimed she was all he needed to make him happy. He loved her so."

"How did she die?"

"It happened when I was just your age. We were out for a ride, when a snake slithered across our horse's path. He bolted. Gittel tried to rein him in, but he'd have none of it. The wagon overturned. I landed in a soft furrow, a twisted ankle the worst of my injuries. My poor sister wasn't so lucky. She was thrown in front of the horse." Tears stung Fruma Ya'el's eyes. She made no attempt to stem them. "Trampled to death."

"And Papa turned to you, his beloved little sister, in his time of sorrow."

Fruma Ya'el coaxed her wooden lips to smile. "Something like that."

CHARLES ROSENTHAL, M.D.

Setting down the tattered diaper she used as a polishing cloth, Fruma Ya'el reached into a concealed pocket in the wooden silverware box's lining and pulled out a tintype of an American physician. He had come to Svechka to persuade young Jewish men to go back with him to study medicine. Lean, with black hair, bushy moustache and olive skin, Charles' image still held the power to quench her arid heart's thirst if only for the briefest moment. The memory of his lips pressed hard against hers still lingered in her mind like sweet cream and honey—their final kiss.

"Charles, I can't."

"You'd rather rot in ignorance because of a narrow-minded old man and a piece of paper than come with me?"

"I'm all my father has left."

Charles' dark eyes filled. He grasped her face with both hands. "I beg of you, Ya'el. Think! There are schools cropping up all over America for women. You'll be an excellent doctor, a medical pioneer."

"What about Papa's honor?"

"Damn 'Papa's honor'!"

PINKAS RABINOVICH

The long winter had come to an end. A new century had begun. Warmed by the spring sunshine, Havah strolled through the streets of Svechka as she and Gittel ran a few errands for Auntie Fruma. In many ways, the town reminded Havah of her Natalya. Perhaps all *shtetls* were the same. Since she had never lived anywhere else, she could not know for certain.

Flowers lined the entrance to the tailor shop. The butcher shop was very much the same, with sawdust on the floor to absorb animal blood. Even the butcher reminded her of the one she had known in Natalya; a burly man with spattered apron and boisterous manner.

"Please sir, I would like to purchase a nice pot roast for the Levines," she said.

His resounding laughter put her at ease. "You must be Gittel's little sister I've heard so much about."

Gittel's freckled cheeks flushed crimson. She wrapped an arm around Havah. "I promise, I've only said good things."

"To any and all who will listen." He laughed louder as he wrapped the meat in brown paper. "Shalom, shalom, dear ladies. Give my regards to your good parents."

The next stop was the post office that doubled as the newspaper office. The postmaster and printer, Reb Pinkas flashed a yellow-toothed smile. Not really a smile, more of a leer that sent shivers through Havah.

She edged closer to Gittel, hoping he would hand them Uncle Hershel's mail and be done with it. He gave a crumpled envelope to Gittel. "Tell your Papa I will be late for Torah study tomorrow. I must put a new article in the paper. The Cossacks have extended their reign of terror." He ogled Havah. "And some of us have felt the edge of their swords."

Tobacco juice oozed from the corners of his mouth and trickled down his crusty beard. *How can someone who professes to be a learned man be so filthy?* Havah wrinkled her nose. *Does he visit the bathhouse more than once a month? I doubt it.*

OREV RABINOVICH

S he's a bargain, this cripple! Not only will she make pretty babies, she can't run far." Reb Pinkas slapped his son's back. "What are you waiting for, boy? Sign already."

Havah clenched her teeth and signed the marriage contract with Orev Rabinovich, the printer's son. *What choice do I have? Arel will soon marry Gittel.* As her legal guardian, Uncle Hershel had the right to auction her off to the highest bidder, like a prized milk cow.

A week later, Orev showed up at the door, flowers in hand. For the first time, she noticed his blue eyes and even teeth. Under his cap his brown hair curled over his ears. "*Gut Shabbes, Fraylin* Cohen."

She learned that Orev was an avid reader. Since he helped his father print newspapers, he kept current with world events. He had much to say and did so with eloquence and emotion. At the same time, he possessed a quick wit and an easy laugh. Little by little, her affection for him grew and her ache for Arel lessened.

Although Orev never discussed social revolution or literature with her, there was no doubt in her mind he would once she shared her secret. She imagined cozy nights by the fire reading and discussing. Man and wife, studying as one. And then, perhaps, they would have a daughter. They would turn Svechka upside down by sending her to Talmud Torah School.

One night in early spring, her fragile hope shattered with the literal turn of a page; when Arel chose the same evening as Orev to call on Gittel.

With his eyes fixed on Havah, Arel picked up her book of *Psalms,* which lay open on the small writing desk by the window. "Orev, my friend, how do you feel about girls reading the Holy writings?"

Orev grimaced. "You're drunk, Reb Gitterman!"

"I'm serious. You profess yourself to be a modern man and a free thinker. What if, let's say, your wife wanted to study Talmud, ponder the words of the Baal Shem Tov?"

Orev turned to Havah and brandished his fist in her face. "I'd beat her within an inch of her life!"

EXILE

Havah's hopes of finding employment in Kishinev dwindled. Disappointed to find the same backward thinking in the city as in Svechka, she limped along the stone sidewalk in the Jewish quarter.

Most of the many shop proprietors preferred not to hire women. The butcher offered to sell her a choice pot roast to cook for her supper. The watchmaker refused to talk to her. And, worst of all, the bookseller laughed at her. "A learned woman? Preposterous."

The dilapidated buildings blocked the sun. Tears clouded her vision. Once more she was a stranger in a strange land.

Guilt riddled her. The Levines loved her as their own daughter and she repaid them by running away. But, she could not watch her beloved Arel married to another. She could not be just his sister-in-law.

"Papa," she whispered, "what should I do?"

"Fight for what you want, Havah. Don't back down and hold your head high."

EVRON AND
KATYA ABROMOVICH

INHERITANCE

"Havah, could you take over for a while?" Katya turned away from the kettle on the iron stove that took up half of the tiny kitchen. She slumped down in a chair, her face as white as her cotton blouse.

Havah grabbed the long wooden spoon from her hand and stirred the porridge made of *kasha* and milk so it wouldn't scorch. "Let me send Zelig for the doctor."

"I'll be fine after I sit for a while. I'm just a little dizzy this morning."

"Up." One-year-old Velvil, dragging his blanket, climbed onto Katya's lap and ringed his arms around her neck.

"You're hardly a baby anymore." She hugged him and pressed her beaklike nose against his tiny one. "My monthly visitor hasn't visited for almost two months. You tell *me*, little midwife, what does *that* mean?"

"Are you sure?" Havah spooned cereal into eight bowls and set them on the table.

While her children scampered into the kitchen to take their seats, Katya winked at Havah with a crooked smile. "I've given birth to five children and she asks if I'm sure!"

When Havah left Svechka a year before, she made a pact with herself. Never would she attach herself to another family. Alas, her plan failed within the first hour of her arrival in Kishinev. Katya and Evron welcomed her as one of their own, but with another child it would be too crowded. Once more the word 'orphan' beat a somber rhythm against her temples.

"I'll find another place to live as soon as I can," said Havah.

Evron burst into the kitchen. Bending down to kiss his wife, he swept Velvil off her lap and hoisted him up onto his shoulders. "You'll do no such thing, Havaleh. We need you more than ever."

"May we have a sister, please? There are too many boys in this house." Ruth and Rukhel chattered like excited squirrels, their words tumbling over each other. "Twin girls like us."

"Having a baby is not like ordering a new suit from your papa, the tailor. We can't tell the Almighty how many stitches to make or how many buttons to sew." With his youngest son still perched on his shoulders Evron sat down on the chair next to Katya. "My precious bride, you've made me a wealthy man. As wise old King Solomon said, '*Behold, children are an inheritance from the Almighty; the fruit of the womb His reward.*'"

THE ABROMOVICH
CHILDREN

LIGHT ONE CANDLE

Twelve-year-old Zelig, the quintessential scholar, pointed to each Hebrew letter on the dreidel. "They stand for 'A great miracle happened there,' Professor Dietrich."

As Zelig's younger sisters, Ruth and Rukhel, set the table, they fluttered around it chirping like excited pigeons. Ulrich could hardly tell where one left off and the other began. Even their voices were identical.

"Hanukkah is all about the Macaroons' victory over their enemies in ancient days . . . It was a miracle . . . The oil in the temple menorah burned for eight whole days . . . That's why we light the candles for eight nights."

Zelig rolled his eyes. "It's Maccabees not macaroons!"

ULRICH DIETRICH

When Itzak suggested to Havah that she apply for the job of housekeeper for Professor Dietrich, a Christian music teacher in Kishinev, she balked. Had she not lost everything to those horrible monsters? Nonetheless, she needed to earn a living and the Jewish shop keepers refused to hire her. What choice did she have?

Far from being the crotchety grey-haired old man Havah expected, Professor Dietrich had thick, sandy hair and a friendly smile defined by deep dimples. His eyes, the same hue as a spring sky, filled with tears when she told him how she had suffered at the hands of Christians.

"I cannot apologize enough for the sins of my people. But I caution you, Havah, not to confuse the word 'gentile' with the word 'Christian.' A true follower of Christ would never do the things these beasts do."

From the beginning, Havah learned two things about her employer. One was his propensity to throw a party for no reason at a moment's notice. The other was his unusual love and respect for her people, referring to them as the apple of God's eye.

THE ARTIST

As the psalmist wrote, "The Almighty puts the solitary in families," so had He given Havah a home with the Abromovich family in Kishinev.

While she loved all five of Katya and Evron's children dearly, seven-year-old Tuli held a special spot in Havah's lonely heart. Rambunctious, and often too noisy for the cramped apartment, his laughter was contagious. Who could be sad around him? Like King David, Tuli was a singer of songs and, like Havah's brother David, Tuli loved to draw. Much to his scholarly brother's dismay, not a scrap of paper was safe from Tuli's creative hands.

One night he crawled into bed with her, his eyes wide with terror. "May I sleep with you, Auntie Havah?" His voice filled with desperation. "I had a terrible dream."

"Tell me about it."

"Monsters . . . they came to our house. They hurt us. You and me. All of us."

"Were they bears or lions?"

"Men. Bad ugly *men*."

"They're gone now." She stroked his dark curls and tucked the blankets around him. "I'll keep you safe, Little Rooster."

He cuddled his head in the crook of her arm. "When I grow up will you marry me?"

GUT SHABBOS

As Havah lit the Sabbath candles, Ulrich remembered how Grandmother lit them every Friday night. When he asked her why, she simply answered, "It was my mother's way and her mother's before her."

Years passed before he understood what it meant for her to be a Jewish woman married to a man who despised her people and had coerced her to embrace his Lutheran religion.

Havah's gentle whisper brought him back to the present. "Ulrich, are you ill?"

Her concerned expression made his pulse race. His tongue stuck to his teeth. "*Nein.* I'm . . . fine. Go on."

Illuminated by candlelight, her hair covered with a lace scarf, she stood at the head of the table, reminding him of a haloed Madonna. Three times she passed her hands over the flames with the fluid grace of a prima ballerina. Covering her eyes, she sang the familiar blessing. Her voice, filled with passion and innocence, caressed his ears like a truelove's embrace.

When she finished, he murmured, "Amen."

VALERICA DIETRICH

As Ulrich's housemaid, Havah enjoyed cleaning his library more than any other room in his mansion. The room was actually a ballroom that doubled as his study. She hoped one day to read all of the numerous books on the shelves that lined an entire wall.

His grand piano took up one corner of the spacious room. Today he rehearsed for a concert, so she tried to be as inconspicuous as possible. The lilting melodies of Chopin lightened her work and she swayed her head in time.

The music came to an abrupt halt. "Havah, do you believe in love at first sight?"

Dropping her feather duster, she spun around. "Excuse me, sir?"

"What did I tell you? Never call me 'sir.'" He pointed to a photograph in a silver frame on the end table beside the piano. A woman with pale curls smiled under a lace bridal veil. "I swear it was love at first sight."

Havah knelt to retrieve her duster. "What was she like?"

"Petite like you. In fact, you remind me very much of her, Havah. How she loved to read! Her favorite subjects were anything and everything. And, like you, she adored children. She could hardly wait until this place was chock-full of our own. But it was not to be. She died in childbirth. Our first and only, our daughter, perished with her." He held the picture to his chest and a tear slid down his cheek. "My Valerica, a woman with music in her eyes."

OVERTURE

A lthough she was his servant, Professor Dietrich invited Havah to sit at his elegant dining table to be waited on like a countess. Not only did he bid her to share his sumptuous meal, but Evron and Itzak Abromovich, their wives and their children as well. What would his aristocratic clients say? Havah guessed he could not have cared less.

After dinner Ulrich led his guests to the ballroom. Itzak and Evron helped him push the sofas against the walls so the children could play or dance without obstacles. It did not surprise Havah that her employer, a concert pianist, should want to serenade his guests after dinner. What did surprise her was to see Itzak and Evron break out their respective musical instruments.

"*Wunderbar!* You brought them." Ulrich sat at the piano and ran his long fingers over the keys, making them trill from low to high notes. "Shall we?"

Itzak raised his violin and tucked it under his chin. "Do one-legged ducks swim in circles?"

Evron held his clarinet to his lips. "At the ready, Professor."

Ulrich waved his hand. "What about you, *Herr Doktor?*"

With an arm slung over the piano's rim, Dr. Nikolai Derevenko, Professor Dietrich's housemate, leaned back in his chair, one foot resting on his opposite knee.

Havah blinked and pointed to the flute in his lap. "So, it was *you* I heard playing all those times!" Up until this moment she had only known the doctor to be straight-laced and aloof. He did not seem to like her any more than she liked him and she avoided him whenever possible. Words stuck in her throat. "It sounded like . . . like . . . angels."

He pursed his lips in a slight smirk. His blue-gray eyes twinkled behind his spectacles. "Surprised?"

"Allow me to explain." Ulrich winked at Havah. "You all know him as a skilled and compassionate physician, but what you don't know is that he is a highly trained flautist and my closest friend since our Heidelberg University days. I hope you don't mind my inviting him to join us tonight."

"A cabinet maker with a fiddle," Itzak plucked his violin strings, "a tailor with a clarinet, a doctor with a flute, and a professional pianist. The perfect quartet."

LANGUAGE OF THE SOUL

Ulrich the concert pianist, Evron the tailor, Itzak the carpenter, and Dr. Nikolai made the most unlikely quartet in Eastern Europe. Piano, clarinet, violin, and flute blended to play "Khosid Dance" with so much energy, Havah could hardly keep her feet still.

Ruth and Rukhel skipped and leaped to the music, chattering and giggling. They stopped in front of Havah and held out their hands.

"Dance with us, Auntie Havah," said Rukhel.

"Yes! Yes, please do," cried Ruth.

Havah shrank back. How long had it been since she had danced? She still remembered the night, three years ago, at Mendel and Fayga's betrothal party. Her brother and his intended were so in love. Once they signed their marriage contract, the musicians played this same song.

Fayga's eyes shone as she squeezed Havah's hand and they danced with the other women. "You're the best dancer in Natalya, Havaleh! I can't wait until we're sisters."

A month later, Cossacks razed the village to the ground, murdering everyone Havah cared about. Although she had escaped with her life, it was not without a price. Frostbite robbed her of her ability to walk, let alone dance.

Havah shook her head. "Cripples can't dance."

"I don't see a cripple, do you Ruth?"

"No, not one here that I can see, Rukhel."

With stubborn insistence, each twin took one of Havah's hands until she stood.

"Just follow us," said Rukhel.

Although her skips were more like hopping limps, Havah kept time to the melody, and even did a clumsy pirouette.

"You're dancing, Auntie Havah!"

In that moment, Havah's crippled heart soared.

PAVEL ALEKSANDROVICH KRUSHEVAN

JOURNALIST, EDITOR, PUBLISHER AND AN OFFICIAL IN IMPERIAL RUSSIA

Ulrich's enamel and silver samovar sat like royalty in the middle of his kitchen table. Steam rolled from its chimney. He poured just enough dark tea from a china pot to cover the bottom of his cup, then turned the samovar's spigot and filled the cup the rest of the way with boiling water. He breathed in the pungent aroma. "Russian tea. The only thing better is strong black coffee from Vienna. Alas, there's none of that to be had here in Kishinev."

Without looking up from his newspaper Nikolai nodded and sipped from his cup. "You could clean wheel axles with that coffee. Give me Russian tea any day."

Ulrich sank into a chair opposite his housemate. "What are you so intent on reading this morning?"

"*The Bessarabitz.*"

"By Pavel Krushevan?"

"The same."

"Kolyah, why do you read such rubbish?"

"'Know thine enemy.'"

"*Touché.*"

"There is an amusing article this time." Nikolai smirked. "Mr. Krushevan actually printed an apology for something he wrote prior to Easter. He accused the Jews of murdering a Christian boy through their ritual, making unleavened bread from his blood. It seems the true murderer has been apprehended, the child's own relative."

"There's nothing amusing about it. One day our Kishinev's going to witness a pogrom like Eastern Europe has never seen because of the outrageous garbage that lunatic writes."

SOULMATE

Fruma Ya'el's skirts clung to her in the summer heat. A slight breeze did nothing to cool her. She sighed. *Who cares about the heat? What difference does it make?* In less than a year, she had lost her husband, her daughter, and her grandson. "I've never felt so alone. The walls are talking to themselves."

Yussel reached over, covering her hand with his. "May I say something? As a friend?"

"Yes, of course."

He coughed, his voice wavering. "We've known each other for a long time, yes?"

"Thirty years."

"Thirty years. I know it's only been six months since Reb Hershel, of blessed memory, has been gone. He was my dearest friend. I miss him, so I mean no disrespect."

Although his black hair had turned white years before and his lucent gray eyes no longer saw, he was still strong and handsome. His cheeks reddened and his grip tightened. "You're lonely. I'm lonely. I'm an old man."

"And I'm so young?"

"I've always respected you, Fruma. My children and my children's children adore you. It's . . . it's been a long time since I've been with . . . a . . . a woman."

"Rabbi, enough with the speech making already!" Her heart raced like a runaway horse. "Yes, I will marry you."

JESUS WEPT

Broken glass, paper and other debris littered the once cheerful apartment. The prophet Jeremiah's words swirled through Ulrich's mind like a hollow wind.

"A voice was heard in Ramah . . .

. . . Rachel weeping for her children . . ."

Dim light from his lantern cast macabre shadows on the spattered walls. He gazed at the children's battered faces and twisted forms. *What could reduce men to such bestial acts?* His stomach convulsed and emptied itself. He wiped his mouth on the back of his sleeve, then cried out, "You bloody bastards! Christ died for you and you use Him as an excuse for your bloodletting! Why? Why? Why?"

CZAR NICHOLAS II

THE LAST CZAR OF RUSSIA

"What are you reading, Kolyah?"

Without raising his head, Nikolai said, "*The New York Times.*"

"You and your newspapers." Ulrich leaned his aching back against the wall. "How are our friends across the sea? Have they discovered a new washing powder to save the American woman from her drudgery? Will their president charge up San Juan Hill again?"

"Far from it. According to this article, Mr. Roosevelt and his Cabinet are pressuring the Czar to denounce the pogrom." Nikolai's voice cracked as he wadded the paper and hurled it against the wall. "Condemn it? No doubt our precious leader is behind this madness. It's one of those things that make me proud to be Russian."

"What else does it say?"

"Read it yourself."

Curiosity aroused, Ulrich scooted to where the crumpled paper had landed. He smoothed it, read the first few lines and gasped. "120 lives were taken and two thousand left homeless. Kolyah, did you read this?"

Nikolai's abject silence answered him. Bowed, with his head against his knees, the doctor's shoulders trembled.

Ulrich turned back to the wrinkled article and read. With cyclonic velocity the words exploded before his eyes. "The anti-Jewish riots in Kishinev, Bessarabia, are worse than the censor will permit to publish. There was a well, laid-out plan for the general massacre of Jews on the day following the Russian Easter. The mob was led by priests, and the general cry, 'Kill the Jews,' was taken up all over the city. The Jews were taken wholly unaware and were slaughtered like sheep. The scenes of horror attending this massacre are beyond description. Babes were literally torn to pieces by the frenzied and bloodthirsty

mob. The local police made no attempt to check the reign of terror. At sunset the streets were piled with corpses and wounded. Those who could make their escape fled in terror, and the city is now practically deserted of Jews."

"During Easter, no less. The holiest day of the year." Nikolai lifted his head and wiped his eyes on his sleeve. "How can those demons claim to be Christians?"

SONG OF SONGS

Arel slid a gold ring on Havah's right index finger. "'Behold you are fair, my beloved, behold you are fair, your eyes are doves.'"

While Yussel recited the traditional seven blessings, she gazed into Arel's clear gray eyes. His clean-shaven face shone like a boy's. She reached up and lightly brushed her fingertips across the scars cobwebbing from his forehead to his chin and whispered, "'. . . my beloved is pure and ruddy, exalted among ten thousand.'"

He cupped his hand around her cheek. At that moment the horrors and disappointments of the past fell away like a worn-out cloak. His breath warmed her face. "'. . . You have captivated my heart, my sister, my bride, you have captivated my heart with but one of your virtues.'"

Her heart palpitating with desire, she replied, "'. . . make haste my beloved, and be like a gazelle or a young stag on the mountain of spices.'"

"Arel!" Yussel shouted.

Arel jumped. "Yes, Papa?"

"You didn't hear a word I said, did you?"

Havah's cheeks heated and Arel flushed crimson. "What . . . what did you say?"

"I said, 'You may kiss your bride.'"

REMEMBRANCE

Trains juddered in and out of the depot. Soon one of those loco-
motives would take Havah and Arel to the pier where they would
board a ship bound for America. Fear of the unknown in yet another
strange land, sadness at leaving her friends behind, and excitement of a
new adventure waged war inside of her.

She turned to see Ulrich having what looked like an unpleasant
encounter with a bear of a man. Ulrich said something and the other
man laughed. Not a humorous laugh. But an ominous one; a sound
she would take to her grave. Quivering with rage, she made her way
through the crowd.

Itzak followed her. "Havah, where are you going?"

Not sure of what she would do or say she stepped up onto an empty
crate and stood face to face with the one-eyed ogre who leered at her
like a ravenous wolf.

"Well, well, who is this handsome young maiden?"

"You don't remember me?"

"Should I, *lapochka*?"

The way his lips curled over his rotting teeth nauseated her. Her
desire to hack him to pieces, one limb at a time, blotted out all reason.
Then, with all the power she could muster, she hit his face with the
back of her hand.

His mouth dropped open and he stumbled backward, lost his foot-
ing, and fell. His head hit the sidewalk with a crack. Blood from his
wound made little rivers between the cobblestones.

A crowd gathered around her and erupted into applause, yet she
felt no sense of victory or triumph. She stepped from her perch and
picked up the cane that had fallen from her weak grasp.

She raised it high, but before she could slam it down across the beast's head, Itzak wrenched it from her. "Not with my masterpiece, you don't."

Undeterred, she gathered what strength she had left and delivered a vicious kick to his ribs.

"*Oof!*" he cried out and grabbed her skirt hem.

Jerking it out of his hand she dropped to her knees and spit in his face. "Suffer and remember, you child murdering bastard."

MOMENT OF MOMENTS

Like an impetuous child, Havah hopped from foot to foot. New York City's imposing skyline appeared to be painted against gray clouds.

What kind of life will we have in this unfamiliar place? She wound and unwound the fringes of her shawl around her index finger. *Will Americans understand my English?*

Yussel grasped her arm. "Is she there?"

"Yes, Papa. Like a queen with flowing robes and a crown, she's standing in the harbor holding her torch high in the air for the entire world to see."

His sightless eyes brimmed and he smiled serenely. "Yes, I see her."

OUT OF THE DEPTHS

Havah gazed out the window, studying the snowflakes. Like milk-white dove wings, they glimmered past the streetlamp and floated to the sidewalk.

"Have you ever seen more beautiful snow, Arel?"

"Snow is snow. It's all the same."

She grasped Arel's hand and held it to her belly. Their unborn child kicked against his palm with such vigor, Havah flinched. Brushing her lips across her husband's disfigured cheek, she fought the stone forming in her throat. One by one, faces of those who had perished before her eyes drifted through her memory.

"No, Arel, nothing will ever be the same."

THE JOURNEY CONTINUES

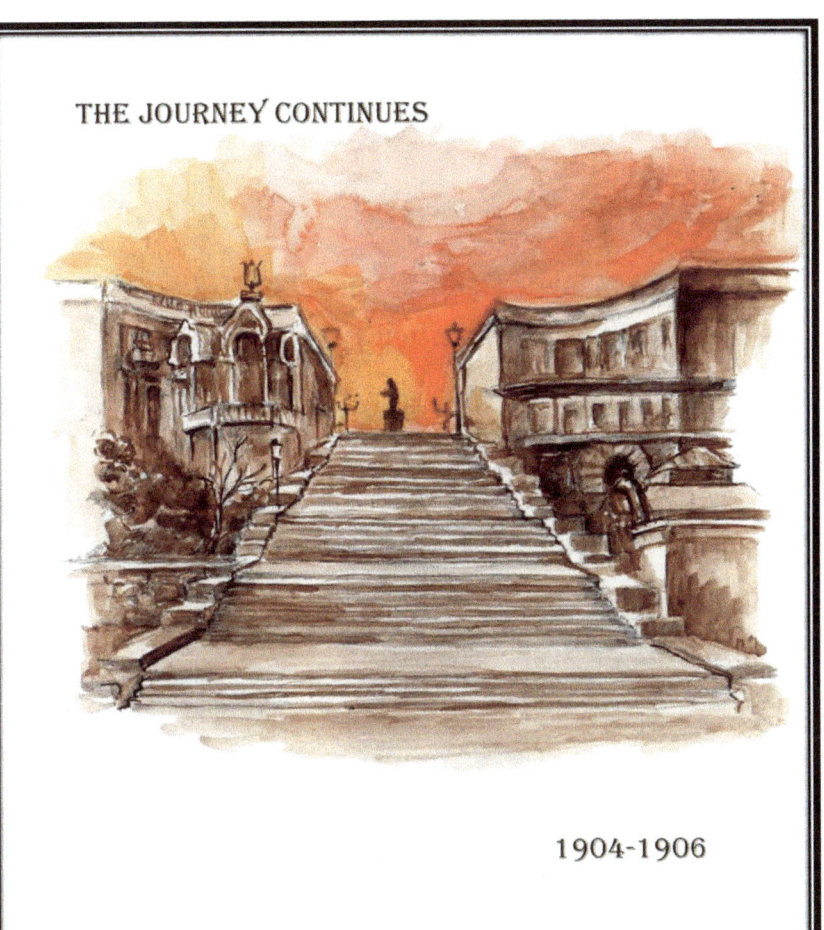

1904-1906

DISTURBANCE

OFFICER PAT MULLIGAN

P olice! Open the door!"

The clock on the mantel chimed three. Havah rubbed her eyes and surveyed her living room. How could she explain the overturned chairs and shattered glass?

"Tell them the truth, Havaleh," said Arel.

"Would you believe me if you were the police?" she whispered.

He pushed her tousled hair out of her face. "I'm sorry I slapped you so hard."

The pounding on the door grew louder. Havah hobbled to it and pulled it open. A sharp gust stung her cheeks. A dour middle-aged woman she recognized as her next-door neighbor stood between two uniformed policemen. She pointed a bony finger at Arel.

"That's him, Officer. He's the one. I'm telling you he's beating this poor li'l gal. I reckon the whole neighborhood done heard her screaming. Jest look at them scars on his face. Any dang fool can tell he's a brawler."

The sight of uniforms terrified Havah. In the old country, uniforms at the door meant one thing. Would these men finish the destruction she herself had caused? Would they haul her gentle beloved off to prison? Or worse, would they kill him outright?

Instead, the taller of the two officers bowed at the waist. "Please excuse the late hour, ma'am. I'm Officer Lafayette Tillman and this is my partner, Pat Mulligan."

"Mr. Gitterman, did you hit your wife?" asked Officer Mulligan.

Arel wrapped a protective arm around Havah. "Yes, but only to wake her up."

Officer Mulligan sneered and pointed to the broken window and blood spatters on the floor. "I suppose you done this to wake her up, too?"

Havah hid her face in Arel's robe. "In my dreams, I do this."

"In your dreams? Like sleepwalking?" Officer Mulligan twirled the end of his moustache. "Yeah, right. I say we take them both down to the station and book 'em. It's as plain as cow plop on your shoe, fighting and disturbing the peace."

MRS. CECIL HUTTON

Havah lay back on the sofa with her dog-eared copy of *Alice's Adventures in Wonderland* propped up on her swollen tummy. She smiled at the drawing of the rabbit dressed in a suit jacket, looking at his pocket watch. How she had laughed when Ulrich suggested she learn English by reading a children's book.

Since settling in Kansas City, she had plenty of opportunity to use her English. Still, English slang daunted her. The words on the book's page blurred as she began to nod off.

A knock at the door startled her. Dropping the book, she rose with some difficulty and patted her stomach. "Settle down, my son."

An older woman, not much taller than Havah, stood on the porch, with a pie in hand. "Good afternoon, Mrs. Gitterman."

"Mrs. Hutton. Good afternoon." *What does the old* yenta *want now?*

"I brung you and your mister an apple pie. Just baked it. Hope you like raisins."

"Won't you come in?" Havah took the warm pie. "*Rozhinkes*—I mean, raisins. They are my favorite."

"Another month, I'd say." Mrs. Hutton patted Havah's belly. "Reckon, it's a girl." She sauntered to Arel's favorite overstuffed chair and eased herself into it. "Raisins is my favorite, too."

Havah set the pie on the coffee table, breathing in the scents of apples and cinnamon. She lowered herself back down on the couch. *Why would this shiksah do such a nice thing for a Jew?*

As if reading Havah's mind, Mrs. Hutton said, "Guess you could call it a peace offering. I feel mighty sheepish reportin' you and Mr. Gitterman to the police like I done the other night. Calling him a brawler on accounta his scars was all kinds of wrong after what them Cossack fellers done to him. And then for you to have them screaming

nightmares." A tear trickled down her wizened cheek. "People killing babies jest 'cause they's the wrong religion or color." She clucked her tongue. "My daddy was a Union soldier. He died fighting agin' such nonsense in the Civil War. So, I hope you'll be accepting of an ole busybody's apology."

Havah reached over and squeezed her neighbor's hand. "Mrs. Hutton, you are welcome in my home any time.

"Call me Aunt Cee-Cee."

OFFICER LAFAYETTE ALONZO TILLMAN

SECOND BLACK OFFICER ON THE KANSAS CITY POLICE FORCE

Havah opened the door and smiled up at the brown-skinned man on the porch. "Officer Tillman, what a pleasant, how you say . . . surprise. Won't you and Officer Mulligan come in and have some *apfel*—apple pie?"

Taking off his hat, he looked over his right shoulder and then over his left. "Pat's not with me. I just came by to make sure you're okay."

"I'm glad. I don't like him." She grabbed his hat and hung it on the hall tree. "I insist you eat some pie. For me it is a *mitzvah*. My sister-in-law is here and wants to meet you."

"Then you're not here alone. Good." With a relieved smile, he wiped his feet on the doormat and stepped over the threshold. "I do love apple pie."

Havah hurried to the dining room table and cut a slice of pie. "Please sit."

With his deep voice and straight posture, his presence filled the room. He sat across from Shayndel and smiled, his liquid eyes shining. "Pleased to meet you, Miss—"

"*Mrs.* Abromovich."

"Mrs. Abromovich." He took a bite of the pie. "Mmmm . . . raisins. Delicious. My compliments to the baker. If I still owned my restaurant, you'd be hired, Mrs. Gitterman."

"*Sheyn Shvartz*," Shayndel whispered.

"I beg your pardon, ma'am?"

Heat rushed to Havah's cheeks. "She said 'beautiful Negro.' You see, before we came to this country I only read about *shvartz*—dark

people—in books. I was so excited to meet you and told my family what a kind policeman you are. Mrs. Hutton, who brought the pie, tells me you used to cut her husband's hair."

"Ah, Mrs. Hutton. I'm happy to see she's made amends. She's really a very nice lady. When I came back from the war in Cuba and reopened my barber shop, Mr. Hutton, God rest his soul, and his friends sang my praises to the powers that be and got me on the police force."

"She says you have a most wonderful singing voice."

"Please tell me she didn't tell you I can walk on water, too."

"You can?"

HOME

Sitting on the porch swing, Havah watched white wisps of clouds against bright blue. She drank in the fragrance of hyacinths and delighted in her front yard. Daffodils, like maidens with yellow bonnets, circled an oak seedling. It was so small, Havah could not imagine it would one day grow into a shade tree.

Spring had come to Kansas City and would soon herald the arrival of her first child. Mama said any day now. Havah hoped for a boy; a son for Arel and a grandson for Yussel, someone to carry on the Gitterman name. Although Arel assured her, since he had grown up as the only boy in a houseful of girls, he would be just as happy with a daughter. Nonetheless Havah planned for a son, a scholar and a namesake for her papa, of blessed memory.

She rose from the swing, waddled down the sidewalk and turned. Looking up at her new house, she grinned. Although it was modest in comparison to Ulrich's Kishinev mansion, it was a palace compared to the crude *shtetl* houses in either Natalya or Svechka.

Her baby leaped and somersaulted. "Oh dear, little Shimon. Must you kick so hard?"

She patted her burgeoning midsection and grinned. With all of her home's modern conveniences, she would never have to use an outhouse again.

THOROUGHLY MODERN HAVAH

Havah piled her jet-black hair on top of her head and brushed it into a stylish pompadour to match the picture in her fashion magazine. Once she had secured the hairpins, she admired her reflection, tilting her head from side to side.

Gone was the peasant girl from the Old Country and in her place stood the up-to-date American woman. She skimmed her fingers over the chic blouse she had bought at Emery Bird Thayer yesterday. Patting a stray curl into place, she grinned with satisfaction. "It's so heavy, sometimes it gives me a headache."

"Is that a complaint or a boast, my beloved?" Arel circled his arms around her waist, his reflection smiling in the mirror. "It would've been a sin to chop it off and hide what was left under an ugly scarf. I hated it when Gittel did. She had such beautiful red hair."

"Didn't she, though?" Havah bristled at the mention of Arel's first wife. "My sister was a slave to tradition, a little like my husband. Arranged marriages. *Feh!*"

Arel frowned. "Must we have this discussion? It's in the past. Poor Gittel died in childbirth. I loved her. You loved her, too. Let her rest in peace." He rested his hand on Havah's round midsection. "We're together now and that's what counts."

Havah whipped around to face him. "Gittel knew it was wrong. She even told me so herself. If you'd done the right thing to begin with and married me in Svechka, she might still be alive."

"If, if, *if!* If Bubbe had wheels, she'd be a wagon."

Tears clouded her vision. "What if I die in childbirth, too?"

Embracing her, Arel kissed her forehead, her nose and then her lips. "Behold, you are fair my love." He pulled out her hairpins and her tresses tumbled to her waist. "Your hair is like a flock of goats."

A NEW AREL

In his youth Arel Gitterman savored his reflection. "Won't I make a handsome husband?"

Papa patted Arel's shoulder. "In the mirror, everyone sees his best friend."

Arel grimaced at his reflection as he shaved and washed the soap off his face. "No best friend here."

He shook his head as he put away his razor. Scars from the Cossacks' beating last year trailed from his left eyelid to his chin and made it impossible for him to grow a beard. Since he lived in Kansas City, it did not seem to matter quite as much as it did in the Old Country. Here, few men, including Jews, sported facial hair, save an occasional moustache or goatee. Even his brother-in-law, Itzak, had shaved off his unmanageable beard.

Tying his necktie, Arel hurried down the stairs to the kitchen. "I have just enough time for a cup of coffee and a bagel."

"It's not like Wolf will fire you if you're late." Havah spread butter on a sliced bagel. "He is your sister's husband after all. Sit. Eat."

"It's my first day. I wouldn't want to make a bad impression." Arel sat and opened the newspaper. "*Oy*, these strange words. I'll never learn them."

"We've only been here three months. With your quick mind, you'll be reading and speaking like you were born here in no time." She sat across the table, love evident in her dark eyes. "After all, you're not just any tailor. You're also a rabbi and a scholar."

Washing down his last bite with hot coffee, Arel stood and put on his coat. "January 2, 1904—a new year, a new job, and soon, a new baby." A tear slid down his cheek.

"Arel, what's wrong?"

"Nothing, my love." He bent to kiss her. "When the heart is full, the eyes overflow."

GOODBYE, HELLO

Picking up a letter from his desk, Ulrich held it to his nose and breathed in the aroma of rose water. He pictured Havah sitting at her table, pen in hand, munching raisins, black waves cascading over her shoulders.

His mind harked back to Rotterdam Harbor where they bid each other farewell. The *Ryndam* would carry her off to America and he would soon board his ship to England. Had it only been four months? It seemed a lifetime ago. The taste of their stolen kiss lingered on his lips, even as her husband, Arel, waited on the dock.

Ulrich's housemate, Nikolai, inspected the envelope. "'Kansas City, Missouri. U.S.A.'"

"The postman delivered it yesterday afternoon."

"What does she have to say?"

"Here, I'll read it to you.

"Friday, 29 January, 1904
Dearest Ulrich, my angel and friend,
Snow is starting to falling here. I am hoping happiness for you. You, above all people, deserve it. You saved my life from the Czar and his horrid Cossacks. I never forget.
I miss hearing you play your beautiful piano. Perhaps one day you will come here for a concert.
Can you understand it, my writing?"

The memory of her battle with her injured right hand still pained him. No longer able to perform simple tasks, such as writing or even holding a spoon, she forced her left hand, with unyielding diligence, into submission. After all of that, she still had impeccable penmanship.

Ulrich tossed the letter to Nikolai. "You can read the rest. She goes on to talk about the family, Arel, and what not."

"I should think you'd be happy for them."

"I'm delirious."

Nikolai squeezed his shoulder. "Ulrich, let her go."

SARAH GITTERMAN TULSCHINSKY

Sarah Tulschinsky, Arel's older sister, fascinated Havah. Her crooked-toothed smile eclipsed her hollow cheeks. Skinny, with a thatch of kinky black hair and round eyes, she lacked Shayndel's physical attributes.

Arel said he could not recall ever hearing Sarah raise her voice, until seven years ago. Always the dutiful daughter, she did whatever she was told until her father arranged for her to marry a man twice her age.

"We couldn't believe it," said Arel. "Even though I was a little boy, I'll never forget the words she yelled at him. 'You may be blind now, Papa. But you've never seen *me.*'"

With that she stuffed her few belongings into a carpetbag. Amid stench and disease in the ship's steerage, she met her beloved Wolf. Married soon after their arrival in New York, they followed their dreams to Kansas City where they lived in a flea-infested shack among the impoverished unwashed in a settlement known as McClure Flats. Side-by-side, she and Wolf established his tailor shop. Within two years, they saved enough money to move from the slums into a two-story home.

Despite all that, Sarah welcomed nine people, one a total stranger, when they arrived from the Old Country. She never complained about her immaculate house being overcrowded. Havah never once heard her utter a cross word, not even with four noisy children underfoot.

"I can never repay you," said Havah one evening as they filled Sarah's parlor.

"It's only temporary." Sarah wedged herself onto the sofa between Fruma Ya'el and Yussel. She squeezed his hand. "Besides, you've repaid me many times over, Havaleh. You've given me back my *mishpokhah*, my family."

WOLF TULSCHINSKY

Havah speared a piece of roasted chicken with her fork. Swirling the meat in a puddle of brown gravy, she clenched her teeth. She did not want to insult Sarah's cooking, but at this moment, hunger was the farthest thing from Havah's mind.

Across the table, Wolf's intense glower made her squirm. While she liked her brother-in-law, she did not care much for his philosophies or opinions.

He gestured to Sarah to serve him another piece of chicken. To Havah's irritation, Sarah quietly obliged him. Without so much as a thank you nod, he continued his tirade. "Are you trying to tell me that you, a mere female, are going to fly in the face of all of our traditions?"

Arel raised his wine goblet. "To my wife, Havah, who is anything but 'mere.' *L'khaim.*"

Havah took a deep breath. "Women have the right to learn Hebrew *and* Torah, but you, Wolf Tulschinsky, would prefer Evalyne learn to push brooms and mindlessly bake bread, kowtowing to her hubby's every need. This is the future you wish for your daughter?"

Wolf slammed his palm on the table causing the silverware to jump. "What would your papa, the revered rabbi, say?"

"My beloved papa, of blessed memory, would say Evalyne's superior intellect shouldn't go to waste."

Sarah switched her pleading gaze from Havah to Wolf. "Please, dearest, we invited Arel and Havah for a pleasant supper."

Wolf leaned back in his chair, crossing one lanky leg over the other, his dark eyes smoldering. "Then tell your little sister-in-law to back off. I am not sending my daughter to Talmud Torah School and that is that."

"Why not, big brother?" Arel smirked. "Are you afraid you'll find out Evalyne's smarter than you?"

EVALYNE AND JEFFRY TULSCHINSKY

With his bat tucked under one arm, Jeffrey stuffed the baseball into his coat pocket. He pulled his cap over his sandy brown curls and yanked one of his twin sister's kinky black braids. "Come on, Evie. Let's go play."

Evalyne's scalp stung. Pencil in hand, she doubled her fist and smacked his shoulder. "I'm not done with my *Alef-bets*."

He stuck out his tongue. "Ugh. I don't understand, Evie. You're a girl. You can't even go to Hebrew school. Why bother?" He squatted and picked up her primer that had fallen off the table. Making a face, he rolled his eyes. "Besides. It's boring."

Evalyne's anger flared. "Boring? It's . . . it's the *lashon kodesh*, the holy language."

"Where'd ya hear that from? Auntie Havah, I'll bet."

"At *shul*, dopey. Maybe if you paid better attention—"

"Aw, you're no fun anymore."

He stepped outside and slammed the door behind him.

The grandfather clock in the living room struck three. Evie held her book to her chest and bit her lip. Papa would be home in two hours. In one hour, Mama would expect her to help prepare supper.

Aunt Havah had given Jeffrey and Evalyne the Hebrew primers for their sixth birthday. She had tucked Evalyne's inside a big bag of books between *Grimm's Fairytales* and *The Wonderful Wizard of Oz* so Papa would not see it. "Why's he gotta be so mean about it? Why shouldn't a girl study *Humash*?"

Rain suddenly pelted the windows and the door flew open. Jeffrey stormed in, leaving muddy footprints on the carpet. "Drat! Drat! Drat!" Dropping down on a chair opposite Evalyne he glanced over at her book. "Hey! You're two lessons ahead of me."

"Want me to help you?"

"Maybe later." He headed upstairs. "I need to go through my marbles. I promised Pete an aggie for a steelie."

Evalyne hunched over her book. "I swear, Jeffrey, when the Messiah comes, you'll be off somewhere else losing your marbles."

ZELDA MAYER

Havah usually looked forward to the ladies' sewing circle on Tuesday mornings at Sarah's house. Although Arel had much more talent with a needle and thread than she, Havah enjoyed socializing with other women in her *mama-loshn*, her mother tongue.

However, today was an exception, thanks to Zelda Mayer who prided herself on her status as a wealthy socialite. All morning, Zelda stitched little and boasted much. She and her husband, Sol, a successful business owner, were going to build a mansion in Hyde Park, a prestigious new Kansas City neighborhood. Every so often, she cast a sidelong disdainful glance in Havah's direction.

"Must you all speak Yiddish?" Zelda's voice grated in Havah's ears. "This is America, you know."

"Remember when Arel and Havah first came to America, Zelda?" Sarah asked.

"Hmph." Zelda hunched over her sewing project.

"Vhat happened?" Mrs. Goldman asked with a thick Polish accent. "I am not hear dis."

"It was last fall." Sarah winked at Havah. "The sisterhood gave a party for my family when they came from the Old Country."

Nettie Weinberg snorted. "Mrs. Hoity-Toity Mayer, thinking none of them speaks anything but Russian and Yiddish, starts spouting her opinions; telling Sarah her '*shtetl* peasant' family is going to ruin her lovely home. Isn't that how you phrased it, Zelda?"

Zelda flushed scarlet and stood. "I don't have to take this." With skirts swishing and heels clicking, she headed for the front door. As she stepped outside, she glared at Havah and Sarah. "Nor will I forget it."

A hush fell as the door slammed behind her. Mrs. Goldman's giggles split the silence. "Finish it, the story, Sarah, in Yiddish so I understand better."

"I wish you could've seen the look on Zelda's face." Sarah grinned. "Havah, my teeny little sister, marches right over to Mrs. Snooty-Punim and says, in English, 'You are nothing but a *shtetl* peasant in a silk dress.' Then she told her off in Yiddish. Of which, I assure you, Zelda understood every word."

SOL AND WENDY MAYER

Daddy, can I ride the Merry-Go-Round again?" Wendy Mayer tugged at Sol's sleeve and whined. "I want to ride Shoot-the-Chutes."

"Whatcha say we grab a big, juicy hot dog first?"

"Yum, Mommy never lets me eat them. She says—"

"Yeah, yeah, I know what your mommy says." Gazing at the sky, Sol mopped his bald head with his handkerchief. Clouds had begun to gather, giving welcome relief from the August sun. "We might be in for some rain. Perhaps we should just go home."

"I wanna hot dooooog." Tears welled in Wendy's blue eyes. Her voice scaled up like a siren making his ears ring. "I don't wanna go hooooome."

He whisked her up in his arms. "*Drey mir nit keyn kop!* Don't twist my head!"

"Ummm, you speaked Yiddish. Mommy says only *shebble* pheasants speak Yiddish."

"'*Shtetl* peasants.' I wish she wouldn't say that. It's not very nice."

Large raindrops splashed his forehead. Sol hastily paid for two hot dogs and carried Wendy to a table. The rain pounded the pavilion's roof.

Sitting her on a chair, he set her food in front of her. "I'll let you in on a little secret. Your daddy came from a *shtetl*."

Wendy dropped open her mouth. "Really? Like the Gittermans?"

"Just exactly like the Gittermans." He took a bite of his hot dog, savoring the taste of sausage, mustard, and bread roll. Swallowing, he dabbed his lips with his handkerchief and then wiped mustard from her chin.

"When I was your age, I lived in a little village called Natalya. *Shtetl* is the Yiddish word for village. We didn't have amusement parks or

street cars like we have here in Kansas City, not even a telephone or a water closet, but we had a swimming hole and trees to climb. And you know what? We were happy." The rain subsided as he took his last bite. "Shall we go on another ride?"

She shook her head. "Huh-uh. Tell me more about when you were a little boy in the *shebble*."

UPON YOUR DOORPOST

Havah traced the Hebrew letter *shin* on the weathered tube on her door jamb with her index finger. The *mezuzah*, decorated with the first letter of the word *Shaddai,* Almighty, was an ancient sign to tell the world a Jewish family dwelled within the walls. It was one of the few things she managed to salvage from the ruins of her village.

She remembered when David, then thirteen, spent hours carving the wood. He had been careful not to crack it as he hollowed out a place to insert the parchment scroll inscribed with verses from the Torah. Havah thought it a pity it would be hidden inside where no one could appreciate Mendel's fine penmanship.

Once David sealed it, Papa proclaimed it a masterpiece and made a ceremony of tacking the *mezuzah* to their doorpost while Mama beamed with pride. How it survived the fire that razed Natalya was nothing short of a miracle. Surely *El Shaddai* Himself had kept it in His mighty hand. Havah brought her fingertips to her lips and kissed them.

With their faces firmly entrenched in her memory, she whispered, "My brothers, Mama and Papa, your words have I hidden in my heart."

DR. NIKOLAI "KOLYAH" DEREVENKO

Anxiety nagged Nikolai concerning Havah's health. Had it not been less than a year since the horrendous massacre in Kishinev's Jewish quarter? Given her size and the extent of her injuries, the pragmatic physician wished she had allowed more time to recuperate before conception. Her frequent letters were filled with happiness and anticipation, insisting she had never felt better. Nikolai doubted her claims.

He slipped a recent letter from Arel back into its envelope. He told Nikolai how she had been very ill with German measles and influenza shortly after their arrival in Kansas City. "Could this hurt the baby, Dr. Nikolai?" Arel had written.

Nikolai put pen to paper. "Although sickness might be debilitating to the mother, my young friend, it is doubtful it will injure the fetus." Nikolai scratched out the last word and replaced it with "baby." He went on to tell Arel about his practice in London. "Like you, I have to speak English. Sometimes it's daunting, but both of us will master it over time." After writing a little more news, he ended with, "Send my regards to your family. I will never forget any of you. As you might say, '*Shalom*,' my friend. Kiss your son for me when he arrives."

While he sealed the envelope, he glanced over at a yellowed photograph of himself with a young child on his lap. "Seven years. Where did she take you, *Solnyshko,* my little son?"

IVONA DEREVENKO

Nikolai leaned back on the sofa and played a somber melody on his flute. The music matched his mood. After seven years he had given up all hope of finding his son. His lonely thoughts turned to the harridan who had stolen him.

From the first day he met her, Nikolai had been smitten with Ivona. With her huge brown eyes and sleek black hair, he thought her the most beautiful woman he had ever seen. After a whirlwind courtship, they married. Nine months later, she gave birth to boy.

Nikolai remembered the night. Her labor was short and their son healthy. His joy knew no bounds.

However, something seemed terribly wrong. Even with the baby in the crook of her arm Ivona appeared to be anything but maternal. She practically threw the baby in Nikolai's lap when he sat, her voice harsh and cold. "The son you've always wanted. I hope you're happy."

"He's perfect." Nikolai took the newborn in his arms with a sense of awe and kissed his soft cheek. "What shall we name him?"

"Name him anything you like." Ivona pouted like a child bored with an old doll. "Can you imagine Dr. Miklos comparing me to a farmer's wife? The very idea!"

"He meant it as a compliment."

"Well, I've never been so insulted in my life. If that's not enough, my figure's ruined." From then on, her obsession with her looks and petulant self-absorption sickened Nikolai. After a year's time, he moved into their guest room. His only consolation was their son to whom she paid little attention. So, it baffled Nikolai no end when she left and took six-year-old Vasily with her.

MARY ALICE TANNER

With a leather portfolio under his arm and his medical bag in his hand, Nikolai wandered London's streets. Since his chief errand was accomplished, he had no particular destination, so he seized the opportunity for an afternoon of sightseeing.

Passengers crowded themselves into square compartments atop coaches whose side and back banners advertised such necessities as Lipton's Teas and Nestlé's Milks. Above all else, London's churches fascinated him with their clock towers. A man never needed to ask the time in Britain.

Now and then, he paused to read shop signs. One particular shop caught his interest with its display of paints and drawing papers. He read the sign aloud, "L. Cornelisson and Son. Artist Colourman."

Suddenly, a flagrant dervish of henna hair and purple feathers in chartreuse skirts swirled past him. Floundering in a wake of strong perfume, he sneezed and opened the door for her. Curious to know what a woman of her ilk would want in an artist's shop, he followed her. He removed his hat, pushed back his straight hair, stepped over the threshold, and shut the door behind him. The pungent aromas of pigment, art paper, and varnish scented the air.

The woman, who had pushed past him, wrapped her fingers around his arm. Her periwinkle eyes sparkled and her crimson mouth stretched into a predatory grin. "I'm Mary Alice Tanner." She pointed to his medical bag with a cackle. "Ain't we met before, Dr.—?"

"Derevenko and, *nyet*, I think not."

"Russian, eh, wot?" The feathers on her hat waggled like flocking birds ready to take wing. Her raucous laughter bounced off the walls and his discomfort mounted. Any moment the buttons of her over-taxed blouse, a scant covering for her jiggling bosom, would spring off.

"I've a friend what talks like you and you does look familiar. You sure?"
She shrugged. "No matter. I'd best be about me business. Can't forget
me little Dodger's birthday, can I?"

"Please to explain. What is a 'Dodger'?"

Her expression changed from vulturous to maternal. "It's what I
calls me nephew. He ain't really no kin to me, but I loves him like he's
me own. Going to be a great artist when he grows up, he is. Thirteen
this next Wednesday."

Nikolai's heart skipped a beat. "My son will be thirteen next
Wednesday."

CATHERINE FLANNERY EPSTEIN

Under a straw hat, her emerald eyes flashed and a profusion of strawberry blonde waves and ringlets bobbed around the young woman's heart-shaped face. Her blouse's lace collar accentuated a graceful neck. "Professor Dietrich, I presume?"

"At your service, *Fraulein*." Ulrich clicked his heels and bowed.

"How dare you give a failing mark to one of the most brilliant musicians of our time?"

"And just who might this 'brilliant musician' be?"

"Quinnon Flannery."

"And you are—?"

"His sister. Mrs. Epstein."

"Yes, it's an unfortunate situation. The truth is, I didn't *give* your brother his failing mark, he *earned* it. Quinnon is talented, but even the most gifted musicians need to put forth a certain amount of effort. The world will never hand out accolades to the undeserving, and neither, *Frau* Epstein, shall I."

Her lips paled and her anger abated like a snuffed candle. She nearly collapsed on one of the red chairs, hiding her face in her hands. "I promised Mum and Dad I'd look after him. See how miserably I've failed!"

Unsettled, he knelt beside her and offered her his handkerchief. "Is there anything I can do to help, *Frau* Epstein?"

"Please call me Catherine." She held out her gloved hand. "I hate the name Epstein."

He lifted it to his lips. "Only if you'll call me Ulrich."

Her round cheeks flushed as she smiled, revealing captivating dimples and a charming overbite. Something about her made him feel as though he had returned home after an arduous journey.

TRANSITIONS

Sitting at the table, Fruma Ya'el enjoyed a late afternoon glass of cold milk with the last piece of apple pie. The buttery crust melted on her tongue. So what if the baker was a gentile and the pie wasn't baked in a kosher kitchen? Mrs. Hutton, Cecil, had been kind enough to share the recipe and Havah had been kind enough to translate it into Yiddish. There was nothing against dietary law in the ingredients—apples, cinnamon, flour, sugar, butter, and, most important, raisins.

Fruma Ya'el popped a bite into her mouth. "When in America, do as the Americans do, as long as it's not immoral."

She relished a rare moment of solitude. Yussel had gone downtown with Arel and she had convinced Havah to lie down for a nap, saying, "Soon that baby will fill your hours with dirty diapers and frequent feedings. Rest while you can."

The fact of the matter was she feared for the girl and her unborn child. Young and strong, Gittel had died in childbirth right before Fruma Ya'el's eyes. In one horrible moment, she lost her daughter and her grandson. Havah's fragile health worried her.

Trying to ease her concerns, Fruma Ya'el rose and took her empty plate and cup to the sink. She turned on the water faucet. "*Oy,* all these modern conveniences, no wonder American women are spoiled. My back aches just thinking about all the buckets I toted from the river. And washing machines! Who ever heard from such a thing in Svechka?"

Fruma Ya'el jumped at a sudden loud ring. Afraid it might wake Havah, she hurried to the jangling contraption on the wall and seized the earpiece. "Some things I'll never get used to." Mercifully, the noise

stopped. "Now, how does this work?" She pressed the earpiece against her ear. "Allo?"

Through crackling static, a strange voice said, "Hello, Mrs. Gitterman?"

She shouted into the transmitter, "Y-ya, I am Mrs. Gitterman, too."

GEORGE WEINBERG

Leading with her cane, Havah limped across the sawdust covered floor. She breathed in the earthy aromas of raw meat mingled with onion and garlic. Her mind traveled back to her precious *shtetl,* Natalya. How she loved to accompany Mama to the butcher shop. In that moment, she was a little girl hanging her nose over the edge of the pickle barrel to catch a hearty whiff.

George Weinberg's loud voice brought her back to the present. "Mrs. Gitterman, what'll it be today? A pot roast fresh from Kansas City's famous stockyard, certified by the rabbi? Or perhaps a chicken for your *Shabbes* table? *Nu?*"

Although George and Nettie had lived in the area for nearly ten years, his New York roots peppered his speech. Havah loved his accent. The son of Polish immigrants, he was a fourth-generation butcher and no one doubted his enjoyment of his trade.

His black curly hair formed a hedge around his otherwise bald head. A stout man in his thirties, his girth made up for his lack of height. With a sweeping gesture, he waved his hand to indicate his empty shop. "C'mon, lady, can't keep my clientele waiting, ya know."

"A roast," said Havah. "And could you chop some smaller pieces for stew?"

He wiped his hands on his bloodstained apron. "Only the finest for my favorite customer." He pointed. "I ain't no midwife, but I'd say any day now."

Havah blushed and tried to cover her burgeoning midsection. George's wistful eyes glittered. "Nuttin' more beautiful than a lady in a family way. Me and my Nettie, we wish we had a house full-a kids."

WHAT THE HEART SEES

Havah gazed at the dark-haired newborn in the crook of her arm. After nearly two days of torturous labor, she was weary, yet too excited to sleep. In awe, she held her baby's tiny hand and studied the paper-thin fingernails. "I was so sure the Almighty would give me a son to be a namesake for my papa."

The baby opened her eyes and formed an 'o' with her lips as if trying to answer.

Arel tiptoed into the room, carrying a vase of daffodils. He set it on the bed stand and lifted the infant into his arms. "She's a beauty like her mama; her mama who should be asleep."

Havah sank back against the pillows and admired the flowers. "They look like ladies wearing yellow bonnets, don't they?"

Arel nodded, but his gaze never moved from his daughter. He frowned. "Havah, have you noticed the way her eyes cross?"

A delicious wave of exhaustion washed over her and she pulled the blanket around her neck. "Mama says it's nothing to worry about. Newborns don't see very well and sometimes they cross their eyes trying to focus. It's normal."

GAVREL WOLINSKY

A world away from Kansas City in Odessa, Ukraine, Arel's nephew Gavrel stood behind his young wife. Steam rose from the dish pan. Sweat beaded Leah's forehead and soaked her kerchief. Gavrel's chest ached with yearning and remorse. She deserved better.

He circled his arms around her waist. "A perfect fit."

Turning in his embrace, she planted a wet kiss on his cheek. "Spoken like a shoemaker."

"How else should I speak? It's what I am. We may not be wealthy, but our children will never go barefoot in winter."

"Remember how angry Havah was at our betrothal. She even accused Mama of selling me into slavery."

"As I recall, you weren't too crazy about marrying me either. After all, I am old enough to be your father."

He surveyed their cramped apartment. With a front room that doubled as a kitchen and three cramped bedrooms, it was much too small for a family of six. Despite Leah's efforts to keep it tidy, it was always cluttered.

"Maybe Havah was right and your mother did sell you into slavery."

"Don't be ridiculous. You give us love and laughter." After another kiss, Leah turned back to the dishes. "I'm happy with my life."

LEAH AND PORA WOLINSKY

Three-year-old Pora, groggy from her nap, crawled up onto Leah's lap. "Tell me a story, Mama."

Leah set her mending in the basket beside the rocking chair. Although she feigned irritation, she relished a rare moment alone with her daughter. The other children, Leah's two younger brothers and little sister, played outside. Gavrel was busy with customers in the shoe shop.

She cupped her hand around Pora's chin. "I'm not as good at telling stories as your papa."

Pora cuddled against Leah. "Tell me a story anyway."

Leah rocked to and fro. "Where should I begin?"

"Once upon a time, of course."

"Okay. Here we go. Once upon a time, there was a young princess with long red hair. She lived in a village far away from Odessa."

"What was the village called?"

"Svechka, which is Russian for 'the candle.' It was a lovely place with tall trees and beautiful flowers. The princess liked to wade in the river behind her grandfather's house and dance at weddings. But one dark day, the matchmaker told her it was time for her own wedding. The poor princess was to marry an old, old man; old enough to be her father."

"Then what happened?" Pora's eyes grew round as wagon wheels. "Did the handsome prince rescue her?"

"No. She cried and cried until she had no more tears."

"Oh, that's so sad. Then what happened?"

Gavrel, who had entered the apartment without Leah's notice, snuck up behind them. Swooping Pora into his arms, he growled. "Crotchety *old, old Prince* Gavrel, who was really a bear, whisked Princess Leah off to his cave."

Pora squealed. "And *then* what happened?"

Leah stood and wrapped her arms around his waist. "They lived happily ever after."

DEVORAH AND TOVA RABINOVICH

Leah's younger sister, Devorah, ladled soup into crockery bowls. "Orev, my husband, all day long you work at your print shop. Must you go to your meeting tonight? Tova and I are lonely. I hardly know anyone here in Odessa."

He scowled and his eyes flashed blue fire. "Selfish *tsoyg*! The blood of our people cries from their graves. It's time for the Jews to rally against the evil Russian tyrants. It's now or never!"

"Are they more important than your wife and children?"

"Children?" Sweeping his bowl from the table, he hollered. "*Klafteh!* You would trap me with yet another little *mamser*?"

Hot liquid soup seared her lap and he smashed his fist into her face. She sank into merciful darkness.

Devorah came to on the floor to a silent apartment. *How can this be happening to me? Just like Mama, of blessed memory, and Papa, may his memory be cursed.* She wiped her mouth and then stared at the red smear on her sleeve. Shutting her eyes, she tried to forget the horrible words he shouted at her, in front of their two-year-old daughter.

The child curled up next to Devorah. Her little finger pressed Devorah's tender cheek. "Ouch, Mama?"

Devorah kissed Tova and opened her eyes. "Yes."

Tova stuck her fingers in her mouth, tears spilling over. "Me, too."

Sitting up, Devorah drew the little girl to her and rocked to and fro. She ran her fingers through her child's crimson curls. "My Little Miss Me-Too. What was I thinking? I should've let him marry Havah. Ha! She was the smart one to run away. Oh, but how I loved him. When did my handsome Orev become an angry ogre? What a stupid little girl I was."

LEV RESNICK

"The bullet nicked the carotid artery. I couldn't stop the bleeding." The doctor removed his stethoscope from his ears. To Lev's surprise, he spoke Yiddish. "How old are you, son?"

"Fourteen."

He pointed to Lev's scarred lip. "How'd that happen?"

"My father's horsewhip. He should rot in the ground . . . as if you care."

Lev dropped down beside the stretcher and stared into Orev's vacant eyes. How could his brother-in-law, his best friend, be alive one minute and dead the next? And such a dishonorable death! Fisticuffs with a compatriot at a self-defense rally led to Orev's death by his own gun. His gray complexion reminded Lev of one of those pictures painted on the outer wall of the Orthodox Church in Svechka. Austere renderings of the man they called Christ repulsed him. Christ, the one the *goyim* claimed he had killed.

Lev pried the gun from Orev's stiff hand and crammed it in his pocket. He wanted to slaughter all of the Christians the way they had murdered his people.

He dropped his head on his knees and wrapped his arms around his legs, longing for his mother, the one person who understood him, filled him, but she was dead.

A tinge of guilt nagged him for the way he had treated his sister Leah since they had moved to Odessa. She had taken on the responsibility of caring for Lev and his siblings and he repaid her with blatant disrespect. He blamed her husband. While Gavrel treated Lev's younger brother and sister like jewels, he treated Lev like a feral cur.

Gently touching Lev's shoulder, the doctor whispered, "Son, no physician on earth could have saved your brother."

Lev pulled away from the doctor's hand and bared his teeth. "I watched you. You didn't try to save him. You stood there and let him die."

The physician's eyes brimmed as he pulled a sheet over Orev's head. "He was a dead man as soon as the bullet penetrated his neck."

"Don't you mean a dead *Jew*?"

VISITATION

Jeffrey Tulschinsky yawned. Would *Pesakh* ever end? If the arguing between Papa and Evie and Aunt Havah was not bad enough, Zaydeh droned on and on about Moses and the children of Israel's flight from *Mitzrayim*.

Last Passover had been much simpler when it was just Mama, Papa, Evie, and him. He did not have to listen in three languages. Jeffrey understood Yiddish because Mama and Papa spoke it, but most of the time they spoke English. But since Mama's family had come from the Old Country, they spoke Yiddish almost all of the time.

"It's only until they learn to speak English," Mama told him.

Aunt Havah spoke English very well, but Zaydeh did not. Even though his grandfather hugged and kissed him often, Jeffrey feared the old man with his unseeing eyes and long white beard.

Zaydeh's voice startled Jeffrey from his daydreaming. "We set a place for Elijah, but alas, I don't see him anywhere."

"Of course, you don't, Zaydeh. You're blind."

Mama's mouth dropped open. "Jeffrey!"

Wishing he could swallow his tongue, Jeffrey hung his head.

"*Oy*, after twenty years my secret's finally out!" Yussel chuckled. "Now, who'll go look for Elijah?"

"I'll go!" Jeffrey raced the other children to the front door. He loved the game. No one really expected Elijah. First to the door, he yanked it open and gasped! "Elijah?"

A tall man with a red handlebar mustache and booming laughter removed his hat and bowed. "I've never been accused of being the great prophet. No, I haven't. Thank you, my boy, I'm Dr. Florin Miklos of

Romania at your service. Is this the Tulschinsky residence? I've been told this is where I might find Arel and Havah Gitterman."

Jeffrey grasped Dr. Miklos' huge hand. "Mama! Papa! Elijah's here and he-he's a gigantic doctor!"

A TIME TO LAUGH

Guilt niggled at Havah for watching Vaudeville at Electric Park on the Sabbath. "What kind of example are we setting for the children?"

"It's too nice a day to be nodding off in a stuffy synagogue." Itzak let out an exaggerated yawn. "Doesn't the *Holy Book* say laughter is good for the soul?"

She grinned at her brother-in-law. His very name meant "he shall laugh." The Almighty must have given Itzak's parents supernatural wisdom. No one could fill a room with cheer and happiness quite like he did.

If meeting him for the first time, a person would never guess how much he had lost in the old country. Nevertheless, the sorrow in his dark eyes since he had lost his brother in Kishinev did not escape Havah's notice. Yet, Itzak rarely complained.

Shaking her head, she turned back to the stage. "You're a bad influence, Big Brother."

Jugglers wearing gaudy costumes spun plates on sticks. Acrobats in skintight outfits flipped in midair. A monkey delighted the crowd by walking on a high wire holding a parasol over its head.

Havah marveled when the magician made a pair of turtledoves appear out of nowhere.

"It's called sleight of hand." Itzak shrugged. "He probably had them stuffed in his trousers."

"Who cares? He's amazing!"

Next the trickster's dog pointed to letters on cards with his paw to spell out his name P-I-L-U.

In a stage whisper, Itzak said, "Good thing his name isn't Constantinople."

THICKER THAN WATER

Havah's lace blouse stuck to her back and her stockings clung to her legs as she pushed Rachel's buggy down the street known as Petticoat Lane. Shielding her eyes with her hand, she studied the skyscrapers that mercifully blocked the summer sun. Even Rachel's whimpers sounded hot and cranky.

"I think Rukhel Shvester's had enough shopping for one day."

"So has her cousin." Beside her on the sidewalk, Shayndel pushed Elliott's buggy with one hand. Her blonde hair hung in her eyes and she fanned her glistening cheeks with her hat. "A glass of lemonade with ice would taste good, wouldn't it?"

"I wish we could go swimming."

"And put this *zoftig* body in one of those skimpy swim dresses? I envy you. Look at you, Havaleh. So teeny. No one would guess you ever had a baby."

Shayndel's words surprised Havah. To her, no one could equal her sister's beauty, outside or in. "It's only been three months. The way your three boys keep you running, you'll have your figure back in no time."

This seemed to satisfy Shayndel. "Itzak says there's more of me to love and that's what's important."

"I'm so glad you came to America. I don't know what I would've done if we'd left you behind in Moldavia."

The shadow of a frown clouded Shayndel's face. "I was so angry when you announced you were coming here. Tell me, would you have come without us if Ulrich hadn't paid our way?"

Havah turned from her piercing glare. From the first time they met, an inexplicable bond formed between them. Yet after the

pogrom in Kishinev, the only thing that mattered to Havah was escape.

Taking a deep breath, she returned Shayndel's gaze. "What do you think?"

FORESIGHT

A myriad of colors danced before Havah's eyes and the room spun with dizzying speed. Somewhere from the miasma, she heard a woman's muffled scream . . . It was her own.

Startled by Havah's outburst, Rachel wailed from Dr. Miklos' shoulder. She quieted as he patted her back and swayed. "She's perfect in every other way. Indeed, she's a perfect child. Try to remember that, Mrs. Gitterman."

"Blind. My daughter's blind." Arel whispered, his voice an agonized rasp.

"It's my fault," said Havah. "I'm a bad mother."

"No, my dear girl." Dr. Miklos smiled sadly. "It happens sometimes and we doctors don't know why."

"Blind." Arel repeated. "Blind."

"She's alive, little brother," said Itzak. "Be thankful."

"Be thankful for *what*?"

"She's been spared the sight of your face."

"Everything's a joke to you, isn't it?" Without another word Arel stomped to the front door and yanked it open. His shoulders drooped like an old man. With his grim eyes on Rachel, he frowned and stepped outside.

Yussel, who had been quiet in his rocking chair until that moment, pounded his cane on the floor. Leaning it against the chair, he stretched out his arms. "Give her to me."

Once the doctor sat her on his lap, Yussel brushed his hands over her face. She, in turn, brushed her fingertips, like tiny feelers, over his nose and lips, grabbed a handful of his beard and cooed.

"The people who walk in darkness have seen a great light." He cuddled her against his shoulder. "*I* will teach her to see."

QUINNON FLANNERY

While Catherine and Quinnon shared familial red hair and green eyes, the similarities ended there. With a perpetual smirk on his narrow face, Quinnon slunk down in his chair and spoke in exaggerated cockney. "Hey, Guv, what's the meaning of keeping me after class?"

Keeping his promise to her to be patient with her baby brother would prove a challenge. To hide his revulsion, Ulrich turned his back to him and rifled through a stack of sheet music. He slipped one from the middle and handed it to the youth. "Here's the piece you'll play for your final recital. It's a folk tune I've transcribed that lends itself well to the violin."

"Yid music? You expect a gifted solo artist to play this Jewish rubbish?"

Ulrich counted to ten under his breath then swung around. His jaws ached with unsaid epithets. Fighting to maintain an even tone of voice, he replied, *Herr* Flannery, your playing is at best—how shall I put this?—adequate."

Quinnon wadded the paper into a ball and viciously flung it to the floor. "Then why should I bother with a recital at all if I have no talent?"

"I never said that. You hit the right notes in all of the right places, but you lack passion. Passion, my good man, is what separates a great musician from an adequate one.

"For example, my friend Itzak Abromovich, without any formal training, plays with such enthusiasm, Antonio Stradavari himself would stand and cheer!"

"All right, then." Quinnon retrieved the sheet music and smoothed it. "I guess I'll give it a go, Guv."

"That's Professor Dietrich to you."

"Being's how you and me darling sister, Cate, is sweethearts, I'd say that makes us mates, eh, wot?"

Ulrich leaned into him until their noses met. Alcohol and stale tobacco odors sent a surge of aggravated nausea through him. "Sister or no sister, you come into my classroom drunk again and I'll see to your expulsion, *personally*."

"You wouldn't dare!"

"Are you a betting man, *Herr* Flannery?"

VASILY DEREVENKO

Unable to concentrate on his newspaper, Nikolai folded it and set it on the table. Ever since Ulrich had met Catherine, Nikolai spent most of his evenings alone. He really did not mind. Catherine seemed just the restorative tonic Ulrich needed.

The doorbell chimed. "Who could that be at this late hour?"

A familiar woman with a henna-dyed pompadour and a determined expression under a feathered hat stood on the step. Her cheap perfume's scent burned his eyes.

How did she found me and why? He bowed at the waist. "Miss Tanner won't you come in?"

"Lord love you, you remembers me!" She stepped inside and whistled through the gap between her front teeth. "Would you look at this place? Why a veritable palace is what this is! Oh, pardon me bad manners, Guv, that McKenzie bloke at Scotland Yard said you lives here." She coquettishly dipped her head, which made the bright feathers on her hat dance. "I shoulda know'd the minute I laid eyes on ya in the artist shop. You looks alike you two."

"Who looks alike?"

"Why you and Dodger, of course."

"Your nephew?"

"Your son, Doctor."

The ground pitched beneath Nikolai's feet. After years of denied prayers and failed searches there stood Vasily on this very doorstep. His eyes seared through Nikolai like a hot poker.

"Eh, now, Dodger." Mary Alice ran her lace-gloved fingers through the boy's hair. "That ain't no way to greet your dad, now is it? At least say hello."

"Zdrahstuyteh . . . Tatko."

NETTIE WEINBERG

After nine hours of agonizing labor, Nettie gave birth to a boy who fit in the palm of the doctor's hand. He lived long enough for Nettie to hold him and sing a lullaby.

The doctor took the tiny corpse, wrapped in his handkerchief. "I'll help George make the arrangements."

As the door shut behind him, Havah sat beside the bed searching for words of comfort for her friend. *What would Papa say?* Nothing came to mind. *Why would the Almighty deny the Weinbergs a child? No one loved children more. Nettie was every child's auntie and could find something to laugh about no matter what. And George? George was just a roly-poly kid himself. Surely, they should have a houseful of noisy, rowdy sons and daughters for him to wrestle with and for her to cuddle.*

"Six months," whispered Nettie. "I carried this one six months . . . five miscarriages. If only my little Myron had lived. Only seven months old when he—"

"You and George had a son?"

"My first husband Avram and I had a son, in Poland. We were so happy, but Avram dreamed of selling his fine watches to wealthy Americans. We managed to save every spare *zloty*—I with my sewing, him with his trade—until we collected enough for our passport and passage. Just enough.

"They crowded us into the cargo hold of the ship; crammed together like so much cattle. *Oy*, can you imagine? Babies and their diapers. Old people. Young people. No place to wash. Sickness. Vomit.

"One day I held my son to my breast, but he refused it. Didn't have the strength to suck. Went to sleep that night. Never woke up.

Avram joined him a few hours later. Cholera. Why, Havah? Why didn't I die, too?

"The Weinbergs took me into their home in the Lower East Side, where they owned a butcher shop. Treated me like a daughter. They provided me with a dowry and a husband, their only son. Not so much to look at, my Georgie, but a good man just the same.

"A year later, we moved from New York to Kansas City. 'Cow Town,' George called it. He heard it's a good place for a butcher and a better place to . . . to . . ." her tearful voice trailed off, "raise children."

SACRED PROMISE

Although he had closed his shop for the day, Gavrel could not go back on his word to finish Reuven's new shoes. He buffed them until they glowed in the lamplight.

Gavrel pulled off his young brother-in-law's tattered boots. "Just in time, Little Apple. Your feet are growing so fast I'd better start your next pair now."

A frown darkened Reuven's ruddy face. "Papa, Lev says someday you'll have a son of your own and won't want me anymore."

Heart racing, Gavrel crushed the boy against his chest. "If I have *ten* more sons, not *one* will ever take your place.

DR. PAVEL "PASHA" TRUBACHOV

Pavel had not changed much since he and Nikolai were medical students in Heidelberg. His wiry frame still seemed to have been constructed of pipe cleaners and his blue eyes had not lost their youthful twinkle.

"I'm sorry about the welcoming committee in the harbor, Kolyah. It's usually more peaceful around here."

Still aching from his violent introduction to Odessa a week before, Nikolai, massaged his bruised side. He studied Pavel's shabby apartment as his sister served overcooked pierogis. She scowled at Nikolai and Vasily before leaving the room.

"I thought you said she couldn't wait for us to come," whispered Nikolai.

Pavel opened his mouth to answer but her voice from the bedroom beat him to the punch. "My brother's idea, not mine."

With a sheepish grin, he cocked his head. "Oxana will warm up to you, you'll see."

Nikolai tried to cut into his pierogi but the fork could not penetrate the leathery dough. "Quite the cook, just like you wrote in your letter."

Pushing his plate away, Pavel licked his lips. "Perhaps I stretched the truth, Kolyah. Would you have come if I hadn't? There's such a desperate need here amongst the Jewish people for medical care. You were at the head of our class, and Dr. Miklos wrote that you've exceeded any surgeon he's worked with."

"I see. You've been stalking me." Nikolai's stomach growled with abject disappointment. "Believe me, I'm all too aware of the Jews' tribulations. I saw it firsthand in Kishinev two years ago. But tell me, Pasha, as I recall, your family had considerable wealth." He pointed to the drab walls. "Did you lose it?"

"We haven't lost it." Oxana reappeared and took their untouched plates to the sink. Her frown deepened. "My brother gives it away and we live like paupers here in Moldavanka with his precious patients."

Pavel shrugged, casting his gaze upward. "It's what my Lord would have done."

OXANA TRUBACHOV

Nikolai rubbed his stiff fingers as he entered the Trubachov's apartment to find Oxana hunched over her embroidery. Her waist-length hair shone like an amber sunset and her thin cheeks flushed as she hunched over her handiwork.

Mesmerized, he watched the needle in her slender fingers glide in and out of the fabric. A red rose appeared before his eyes.

"What's it going to be?" he asked.

"I haven't decided. A blouse, perhaps, or maybe a dress."

"It will be lovely on you either way."

"You needn't flatter me, Doctor. 'She's plain as a slice of bread' my father used to say."

"And you believed him?"

"I have a mirror." She set her sewing aside and pointed to the floor at her feet. "Come here. Sit."

"How can I resist such a tender invitation?"

"I mean, that is, you look tense. Let me massage your shoulders for you. I do the same for Pasha after he's spent long hours in surgery." She held up her empty hands, palms out. "No weapon."

"What makes you so sure I've been in surgery?" He stripped off his waistcoat and sank to the floor. "Perhaps I've been with a lady friend."

"You hate women as much as I abhor men." She plucked off his spectacles and set them on the table.

Closing his eyes, he leaned his head against her knees. "The operation was a success."

HONEYMOON

The full moon's reflections flickered on the waves like radiant sea creatures, or sequins under a spotlight. A salt laden breeze ruffled Ulrich's hair. He relished the cool ocean spray on his face and the warmth of the woman in his arms.

Catherine leaned her head on his shoulder. "I've never known such happiness, dearest."

"Nor I, Mrs. Dietrich."

"Are you excited to see your old friends in the States?"

He squeezed her waist. "Very."

"Not so hard, my love." She turned in his embrace. "I can hardly breathe."

The moonlight shone in her emerald eyes. One by one he pulled out her hairpins until her auburn hair tumbled around her shoulders. Sweeping her up into his arms, he whispered in her ear. "*Meine liebling,* I'm going to lick off every one of your freckles."

Filled with urgent desire, he carried her into their cabin and laid her on the bed. Giggling, she helped him unfasten her dress and corset. He untied his necktie and tossed in the floor, along with his waistcoat. She slipped her hands inside his shirt before he could unbutton it. Her hot breath in his ear made him tremble.

"Ulrich, darling, may I ask you something?"

"Anything. For you the answer's always 'yes'."

"Do you still have feelings for Havah?"

MIDNIGHT SERENADE

Rachel's cries from the next room woke Arel from a pleasant dream. He groaned. "What now?"

Beside him, Havah moaned and wrapped her pillow around her head. "It's her tooth. Again."

He yawned and stretched. "Let me."

"You need your sleep," she mumbled. "You have to go to work . . . tomorrow . . . mmm . . ."

"No, I don't. It's New Year's Day."

Donning his robe and slippers, he stood. In the dim light, he could see that she had already fallen back to sleep. He tied his sash as he tip-toed across the hall to the baby's room.

Standing in her crib, fingers in her mouth, in his presence, her cries subsided. "Poppy."

Arel marveled. Although she could not see, at ten months, Rachel's remaining senses served her well. Taking her in his arms, he held her against his shoulder. "Let's go downstairs so Mama can sleep, shall we?"

"P'nano?"

In the front corner of the living room, Arel sank down on the piano bench with the baby on his lap. Light from the streetlamp poured through the bay window illuminating her black curls. She reached out her tiny hands like antennae to find the keyboard. When she did, she lightly tapped the keys and played a few low notes. Her mouth spread in a four-toothed grin. "P'nano."

"1905," he whispered. "What will this year bring, my clever daughter?"

Memories flooded him. Could it have only been two short years ago his first wife Gittel died giving birth to their stillborn son? Months

later he and Havah cheated death in Kishinev. Now married, they lived in the land of the free and the home of the brave.

Brave? This in no way described him. He had nearly turned his back on his own child because of her blindness. *What kind of father does that?* Yet the Almighty continued to bestow blessings on him: a beautiful wife, employment and a comfortable home.

"I don't deserve this."

"Poppy." Rachel snuggled against him. "Love Poppy."

"Any of this."

BERYL MAYOROVICH

At the end of the school day, nine-year-old Havah closed her textbook. She gathered the rest of her books and papers. Ten-year-old Beryl Mayorovich stopped at her desk and yanked one of her long braids. With a leering grin, he crunched a peppermint stick. "You're really smart, Havah Cohen. Too bad you'll never be anything more than somebody's wife." His candy hung out the corner of his mouth like a red and white striped cigar. "Ha! You might even be *my* wife."

Hands on her hips, she stuck out her tongue. "I wouldn't marry you if you were Adam and I was Eve!"

Yet by the time he turned thirteen, he had grown at least three inches. His round chin had squared in anticipation of manhood. The sight of him no longer repulsed her, nor did the idea of becoming his wife.

One sunny afternoon, holding hands with him under a tree, twelve-year-old Havah pledged her love. But shortly after she turned fifteen, Beryl's father announced his plans to leave Natalya.

Behind the synagogue, Beryl kissed her cheek. "I promise, Havaleh. When I have the money, I'll come back for you."

She tucked her hankie into his pocket. "I will wait, even if it takes forever."

Cossacks, death, and distance broke their childish promises. Six years later, life in America as wife and mother kept her mind occupied. Her heart belonged to her beloved husband, Arel. Beryl's memory faded into the past.

Who could have imagined he would show up in Kansas City? Yet there he stood before her, broom in hand, in Mayfair, his uncle's dry goods store, a world away from Moldavia. He might have changed his

name to Barry Mayer, but the lopsided grin and mischievous eyes had not changed.

He pulled her yellowed hankie from his pocket. "Havah, is it really you?"

CONNECTED BY LOVE

The aromas of savory pot roast and cinnamon rolls hung in the air of the Weinberg home. Havah's heart welled with joy for her friends on the adoption of their son. Eight days old today. She hugged Nettie who greeted them at the door, her baby in her arms, and led Havah to the sofa.

"I'm happy to see you up and around, Havaleh. You still look pale." She pointed to Havah's cheeks. "I've never seen anyone die of chicken pox, but for a while I feared you would. Sit."

Havah tried to cover the ugly scabs with her hand. "I can't thank you enough for caring for Rachel."

"She's no trouble and Kreplakh adores her."

"Kreplakh?"

"You know, the puppy George brought home last year. My substitute child. Ha! That flea bag has done nothing but whine since your precious daughter went home."

"I wish I could've been at shul this morning for the *bris*. Benjamin's a good name. It means 'son of my right hand.'"

"There was nothing to see." Nettie shrugged. "A little snip and it was all over. Benjamin slept through the whole thing. It'll mean more to him when you come out for his bar mitzvah." She lay the squalling infant in Havah's arms along with a warm bottle. He nuzzled Havah and latched onto the rubber nipple. "Always hungry this one."

His warmth and mewling sounds lulled Havah. She had almost drifted off when she heard Itzak say, "Would you look at that! Rukhel Shvester's walking!"

Havah's breath caught in her throat. With one hand grasping the scruff of Kreplakh's neck, Rachel toddled toward her on two feet.

"Keppy, go Mama." When she reached her destination, Kreplakh licked Rachel and sprawled out on the floor so the girl could use her as a step stool.

Nettie whisked the baby off Havah's lap to make room for Rachel. "Havah, I don't suppose you want a dog?"

"Do I have a choice?"

FOR SUCH A TIME
AS THIS

Not one corner of the synagogue hall was left undecorated. The linoleum floor, polished to a high gloss, and the freshly painted walls reflected the glow of the brass light fixtures. Paper chains crisscrossed from one corner to the other. Childish paintings adorned each wall, commemorating the victory of the Jews over wicked Haman in Shushan in ancient Persia.

The stage had been set at one end of the hall. With Wolf's help, Itzak had built a small, yet convincing, palace. Two little faces with red noses peeked through the painted cardboard windows.

"Mendel, David, that castle is for the play." Itzak's laughter bounced off the high tiled ceiling.

"But we want to be in the play, too." David pouted.

"Tell you what." Arel winked at Itzak. "You boys can be my chief noise makers. Whenever it's time to boo Haman, I want you to jump up on the stage and make your groggers roar. Can you do that?"

David clapped his hands. "Yes, Uncle Arel. We'll be the best chief noisemakers that ever was!"

In the past month, Arel and the children had been working on a reenactment of the "Book of Esther" for Purim. Zelda insisted that her Wendy play the lead role. After all, the Mayers gave the most money to support the synagogue. With some resistance, Arel accepted the rabbi's edict and cast Wendy as Esther, the Jewish girl responsible for freeing her people from Persian tyranny centuries before.

"You're a beautiful Queen Vashti, Evie." Havah righted Evalyne's skewed crown.

"It's not fair. I wanna be Haman, but Uncle Arel won't let me." Evalyne jutted out her lower lip. "I wish I was a boy."

Wearing an extravagant evening gown, with a glittering rhinestone

tiara in her hair, Zelda entered the room waving her arms like a reigning monarch in a parade. "Make way for Queen Esther!"

Behind her, wearing a matching gown and tiara, Wendy whined and dragged her patent-leather clad feet.

Havah rolled her eyes. "Leave it to Zelda Mayer to make a children's Purim play into a high society social event."

BEND IN THE ROAD

The romantic notion of touring the States had already lost its allure amid trains, carriages, misplaced belongings, sleepless nights, hurried concerts, and pretentious soirees. Lulled by the summer breeze and the clop-clop of horses' hooves on the dirt road, Ulrich fought to keep his eyes open.

At Catherine's insistence, he'd submitted to a day trip from Boston to Wrentham. The night before, after his concert, she and a Mrs. Macy had arranged it. Although he had no recollection of the exchange, Catherine maintained that he cheerfully consented. He only wished her annoying brother had stayed at the hotel.

The carriage stopped in front of a three-story house with a balcony and screened-in porches on two sides.

"Perhaps they can suggest some resources to pass along to the Gittermans for their little Rachel," said Ulrich.

Quinnon sneered. "Always looking out for your concubine and her blind brat, eh, Guv?"

A stout woman with dark eyes bustled toward them, her hand extended. "Professor and Mrs. Dietrich, how lovely of you to come. Helen and I are delighted."

"It's wonderful to see you and your amazing prodigy again, Mrs. Macy." Ulrich bowed and kissed her hand.

"*Guten Morgen*, Professor." A young woman with chestnut hair and pleasant smile followed Mrs. Macy. Although she was obviously blind and deaf, and her high-pitched monotone was hard to understand, he marveled at her poised self-assurance. She held out her right hand.

He bent to kiss it. "My pleasure, Miss Keller."

At her side, a Great Dane let out a low growl. With a ferocious bark he lunged at Quinnon and pinned him under his paws. Quinnon writhed and screamed. "Get this bloody beast off me!"

"That's odd. I've never seen him exhibit such aggressive behavior." Mrs. Macy grabbed the dog by the collar. "I apologize. He seems to have taken a dislike to you, sir."

"Smart dog," whispered Ulrich.

I WILL BETROTH YOU TO ME FOREVER

Nikolai left the Wolinsky's apartment with a single thought, *I have to talk to Oxana*. Who could blame her for being upset? Oh, why had he been such a *durak* and blurted out his intentions to join Dr. Miklos' practice in Kansas City to everyone before speaking to her? He had been the brunt of her snide remarks, which he took in stride, but her heartbroken sobs seared him.

He grabbed her arm. "Oxana, please."

With her fingernails clawing chunks of his flesh, she pried off his hand. Once free, she redoubled her pace. "Pack your bags. Get out! Go to your Kansas City and be a big time American doctor."

He raced her to the apartment entrance. She grasped the handle, but he slammed his palm against it the door. "Damn you. You are the most insufferable, impossible, disagreeable woman I've ever met."

She spun around to face him. "You left out dull, dowdy, and ugly."

He shoved her and pinned her shoulders to the wall.

She writhed and screamed. "Let go of me!"

"Not until you give me an answer."

"To what?"

"To this." He pressed his mouth hard against hers.

She turned her head and slapped him. He tightened his grip and kissed her again, deepening it until her shoulders went limp. He pulled back and gazed up into her eyes.

"Oxanochka, come with me to America."

"Are you asking me . . . to . . . to marry you?"

"I'm not asking. I'm begging."

CHIEF OF STAFF

"Rollo, come back here!" Quentin raced the St. Bernard down the long hallway but could not catch him. "No, Rollo. Papa's working."

The dog galloped into the office and went straight for Papa at his desk. Nearly knocking over the chair, Rollo leaped up and licked the man's face.

Papa slipped off his smeared spectacles and scratched the dog's ears. "Bully, my canine friend. What mayhem and frolic have you and my good bad boy, Quentin, wrought this fine day?"

Seemingly pleased with himself, Rollo sat back on his haunches and laid his head on Papa's lap. Beside the chair sat a cardboard box full of stuffed bears. Papa rolled a coin between his fingers.

"What's that?" asked Quentin.

Placing the coin in Quentin's hand, Papa pointed to the Russian letters. "This, my son, is a ruble."

"Who's the man on the front?"

"That is Czar Nicholas . . . an evil tyrant."

"Why do you keep it if he's so terrible?"

"To remind me of a young lady I met two years ago at Ellis Island; a proud woman of Jewish heritage. Eyes like a little fawn that could melt the stoniest heart. Poor girl was left a cripple by the Czar and his miserable henchmen. Sharp wit. Indomitable spirit. She came from Russia with her family to settle in this great land of ours. Never take it for granted my boy."

Papa took back the ruble and stuffed it into his vest pocket. "As a matter of fact, I'm sending these fine Teddy bears to their children. Would you like to help me package them for their journey to Kansas City?"

"Yes!" Quentin picked up a framed photograph from the box. "This isn't a bear, Papa, it's you."

"That's my scamp of a son. Now that you're seven, can you read it?"

"*To Havah Gitterman, an Am-er-ic-an woman of val-or. Best wishes from your friend, Theodore Roosevelt.*"

BAYLA RESNICK

Leah put the final touches on a ruffled pinafore and held it up to Bayla. "Won't you be a pretty little traveler?"

Bayla dropped open her mouth. "I love yellow."

"Sunny, like my baby sister, the chatterbox." Leah folded the garment. "We'll save this for our journey to America. New clothes and a new home."

"Will we be in Kansas City on my birthday?"

"Yes. I can't believe you're going to be six already. Soon you'll be too big for cuddling." Setting her sewing on the table beside her, Leah gathered Bayla onto her lap. "Your Auntie Havah helped Bubbe Fruma bring you into the world. I can't wait to see them."

"Do they know we're coming?"

"Of course, they do, silly. And they're already making plans for your birthday party. What do you want for a present?"

Bayla's eyes glowed and she tapped her index finger against her rosy lips. "I want a blue hair bow and a new doll with hair like mine."

A sigh escaped Leah's lips as she studied her little sister. Unlike Reuven, Devorah, Lev and herself, with their red hair and brown eyes, Bayla's eyes were gray and her curls black as coal. She crushed Bayla against her chest.

Squirming in Leah's embrace, Bayla reached up and wiped a tear from Leah's cheek. "You're thinking about Mama, aren't you?"

"You look so much like her."

Bayla sucked in her lower lip. "Is that bad?"

"Oh, no. She was beautiful. Like an angel."

Laying her head on Leah's shoulder Bayla whispered, her breath

sweet and warm on Leah's neck, "What do you think Mama would say if she were here?"

"She would say . . ." Leah stroked Bayla's cheek. "She would say, 'Go away closer.'"

INQUISITION

After news of the pogrom in Odessa swept through Kansas City, area rabbis brought all of their congregations together for a meeting. The intention had been to form a union against violent anti-Semitism in Eastern Europe. Instead, the gathering ended in a shouting match.

Yussel choked on rising bile as he listened to the voices of people pouring from Keneseth Israel Synagogue. Some argued. Some wept. He cleared his throat and whispered, "Fifty-nine years and nothing has changed."

Arel linked arms with him. "Let's go home, Papa."

"Home. Where is that? We Jews have no such place. Tossed from pillar to post. Always strangers in strange lands."

"This is America, Papa. We're safe."

"Safe? How long before. . . ?" Yussel's mind traveled back. Once more he was five-years-old. "My *Yosi*, she called me, even as she died like a dog in the street."

"Don't Papa."

"My father promised me the Almighty would protect us. Ha! I still see my Zaydeh, my grandfather, of blessed memory, weeping in the *shul*. Torah scrolls unraveled and torn from their rollers. Books shredded. Prayer shawls ripped to pieces like any other *shmata*. Now my grandchildren. Why, Arel, why?" Yussel pressed his palm against Arel's face. Tears that made crooked rivulets between the scars ridging Arel's cheek bathed Yussel's fingertips. "I'm sorry, my son. Let's go home."

NIGHT TERRORS

Nikolai clung to the deck railing, his stomach churning with the water. Overhead, storm clouds gathered and rain doused his night-shirt. Swells grew as they approached the ship's hull. Foam capped the rolling waves. Lightning streaked the sky, momentarily blinding him.

"Kolyah! Have you gone mad?" He turned to see Oxana, her long hair blowing around her shoulders in the doorway. She pulled her dressing gown around her and shouted over a crash of thunder. "Come back inside."

Shivering, he sloshed through puddles. "I needed some fresh air."

"Look at you, barefoot and practically naked." Once he was inside, she helped him peel off his wet clothes and put on a dry gown. "Please come back to bed."

"'To sleep, perchance to dream?'" He glared at her. "*Nyet!*"

"Then eat something. I saved your dinner. You hardly touched it."

He sank into a chair and listened to the roiling sea. The images in his nightmares flashed through his mind. "I can't, Oxana. I can't."

"You're burning up, Dr. Derevenko." She pressed her cool palm against his forehead. "What can't you do?"

"Gone like steam from a samovar." He hunched over and dropped his head into his trembling hands. "I couldn't save them."

"No one could have. You're a doctor, my husband, not God."

"Not anymore."

"But Dr. Miklos in Kansas City is counting on you to join his practice."

"He'll have to find another surgeon. *Dorogoy Bog na nebesakh,* dear God in heaven. After wading through the blood of children, how can I ever cut into human flesh again?"

THE JOURNEY ENDURES

1907-1909

MISS KLINE

Afternoon sun streamed through the tall classroom windows and cast long shadows across the dusty floor. On the chalkboard in rigid script was written, "9 October 1907, Wednesday." Arithmetic problems in childish scrawls covered another blackboard on the opposite wall. Behind her desk, the fifth-grade teacher sat with rawboned fingers clasped on top of her attendance book. Her hair was parted down the middle and pulled back from her face into a severe bun.

Under the teacher's spectacled glare, Havah fidgeted on the hard chair. "What did my Reuven do that was so terrible?"

"He gave another boy a black eye."

"Reuven says the other boy hit him first."

"I don't care who started it. Fighting will not be tolerated in my class, Mrs. Gitterman, and that is that."

"He says the other children are mean to him. They call him names. They call him 'Liar' and 'Gravedigger.' Can't you make them stop, Miss Kline?"

"Yes, they do. But he's partly to blame for this I'm afraid. He tells the most outrageous stories. And what he writes for his assignments . . ." The teacher clucked her tongue. "I had the children write a poem called 'Autumn Comes to Kansas City.'" She lifted a page from a stack of papers. "This is what your son wrote.

"'Autumn comes to Kansas City
Orange and golden trees make me sad
Far, far away in a graveyard
The dead girls can't see them.
They used to dance in the leaves
Now they lie ever so still in the dirt
and wait for snow.'"

REUVEN RESNICK GITTERMAN

I fear Reuven has a morbid fascination with death." Miss Kline leaned forward and peered at Havah as she slipped a paper from the folder on her desk. "I asked my kids to write an essay about their hero. Most of them wrote about their mother or father.

"It's not unusual for boys to make up adventure stories, especially when the truth is less than exciting. One of my students writes his father is a cowboy. What an imagination. I know his father, a mild man who works at the meat packing plant. But what your son wrote is beyond adventure."

The teacher read in a low, strained voice.

"'My Hero' by Reuven Gitterman

"I will never forget the day my Papa the shoemaker saved my life. It was morning. We had just finished breakfast. My sisters were washing the dishes when some bad men pushed open the door of our apartment above the shoe shop.

"Bang! Papa shot two of them. They fell dead. But there were too many, and they killed my sister Leah, then they shot Papa. When I ran to him he grabbed me and made me lay down on the floor. Then he fell on top of me. He said, 'Be very quiet, Little Apple.'

"I pretended to be dead. I heard gunshots and the babies cried.

"Then they stopped and it was quiet. Dead people quiet. Papa stopped breathing. I could feel his warm blood on my back. The only ones left are Lev and Bayla and me.

"I will never forget Papa. My hero.

"The end."

"You see why I urge you to have a talk with your son, Mrs. Gitterman? Your husband is very much alive. Why would your son write this pack of lies?"

Anger boiled in Havah's chest. She slammed her palms on the desk and leaned into the other woman's face until the tips of their noses almost touched. "You will apologize to my Reuven. He is no liar."

MISS TOVA

Havah sat beside Bayla on the porch swing and mused. *How could it be November and feel like spring?* What her neighbor, Mrs. Hutton, often said of Kansas City proved to be true. "If you don't like the weather here, jest wait a minute."

Bayla leaned against Havah and grinned up at her. "Miss Tova says she likes 'just us' days, Mama."

Havah took the doll from Bayla's lap and smoothed her hair. "Do you now, Miss Tova?"

Two years had passed since Arel and Havah had taken in and adopted their niece and nephews who had survived the massacre in Odessa. It did not take the boys long to learn English and rise to the top of their classes in school.

Bayla was another story. For the first few months, the child reverted to infant-like behavior, refusing to use the toilet and sucking her thumb. What worried Havah most was Bayla's mute silence. Dr. Miklos assured her that when the girl felt safe, she would come back to her six-year-old self.

For the most part, his predictions had come to pass. Bayla returned to being a chatterbox and had made many friends in school, yet she continued to carry Miss Tova everywhere. Every time she spoke, the conversation began with, "Miss Tova says . . ."

What if Bayla took Miss Tova with her to her marriage canopy? Although the doctor instructed Havah not to push the child, she decided an occasional nudge might help.

Holding the doll to her ear, Havah nodded as if listening. "Miss Tova says you're almost eight, Bayla. You don't need her to speak for you. Uncle Arel and I will make sure no one hurts you ever again."

Bayla's smile faded. "And no one will hurt you or Rachel or Lev or Uncle Arel or—?"

"Promise."

Taking the doll from Havah, Bayla cradled it in her arms. After a few moments of thoughtful silence, Bayla cuddled against Havah. "Miss Tova says she loves you."

RACHEL ESTHER GITTERMAN

Reuven's teacher did not appear to be nearly as austere and threatening to Havah as she had weeks before behind her school desk. Her light brown eyes shone in the candlelight and she flashed a pleasant smile. "Thank you for such a lovely supper, Mrs. Gitterman. I usually eat a sandwich on Sunday evenings while I grade papers." Miss Kline pulled a leather-bound book from her bag beside her chair and handed it to Reuven. "I've enjoyed your hospitality so much I almost forgot the reason I came in the first place."

"Thank you." Reuven opened the book and his forehead puckered into a puzzled frown. "The pages are empty."

"It's a journal. You're a gifted storyteller, Master Gitterman. I suspect you'll have those pages filled in no time."

"May I see the book?" asked Rachel.

Miss Kline glanced at the girl, and quickly looked back at Havah. "She's—"

"I'm blind. Dr. Miklos says I don't have any floppy nerves."

"*Optic* nerves," said Havah.

"I'm this many." Rachel held up three fingers and then raised another. "I'll be this many in March. Wanna hear me play piano? May I, Mommy?"

"Always. Play something pretty."

Kreplakh rose up on all fours beside Rachel's chair as she grasped her halter. The dog led Rachel to the upright piano in the living room and lay down next to it. Using Kreplakh as a stepstool, Rachel climbed onto the bench and lifted the lid.

"Surely you don't allow her to bang on that lovely instrument?" whispered Miss Kline.

Havah smiled but said nothing until Rachel danced her tiny fingers across the keys in a playful melody.

Miss Kline clapped her hand over her mouth. "Bless my soul, it's . . . it's . . . Bach's 'Musette'!"

MENDEL AND DAVID ABROMOVICH

Havah stood at the bay window in her living room. In the front yard, seven-year-old twins, Mendel and David, tossed a baseball back and forth. Mendel squealed when it went over his head and he fell on his bum trying to catch it. Havah grinned. Those two boys held a special place in her heart. Not only had she helped Fruma Ya'el deliver them, but Shayndel and Itzak honored her by naming them after her brothers who had been murdered only months before.

"It's hard to tell they're brothers, let alone twins," she told Shayndel. "Different in so many ways."

"And what one doesn't think of, the other one will."

"Just like my own brothers. It's as if Mendel and David Cohen live on through their namesakes."

Dark-haired Mendel was already a scholar and the joy of his second-grade teacher, while golden-haired David preferred athletics. Unlike his studious brother, David enjoyed teasing the girls in his class or disrupting arithmetic lessons by making up silly songs about numbers."

Shayndel pressed her forehead against the glass. "What do you suppose they'll be when they grow up, Havah?"

"Good men."

ELLIOTT AND TIKVAH ABROMOVICH

Shayndel inclined her face over a steaming kettle and breathed in the fragrance of onions and chicken. "Mmmm. Lunch is ready."

Two-year-old Tikvah tugged at Shayndel's skirt. "Me taste?"

Itzak burst into the kitchen, wrapped both arms around Shayndel's waist and planted a loud smooch on her cheek. "Me taste, too, Mama?"

"Ugh!" Sitting at the table, Elliott made a face and bent over his drawing. "Mushy."

"Now, I'll gobble my golden-haired princess!" Scooping Tikvah up in a bear hug, Itzak growled. "Sweeter than Bubbe's sponge cake. Num! Num!"

Tikvah squealed as he lowered her into her highchair. Shayndel ladled soup into bowls and set them on the table. She snapped up Elliott's crayons and stared at the sketch. "What's this going to be?"

"It's a flower and the grass." He flipped the paper. "You gots it upside down. That's better. See? It's a present for you."

Tilting her head, Shayndel studied the green, pink, and yellow scrawls. She kissed her three-year-old son's nose. "Thank you, sweetheart. It's perfect."

ANDANTE

Nikolai scanned his music history students' faces. Expressions ranged from mild interest to abject boredom. He closed his book. "That will be all on Frederick Chopin for today. Unless there are any questions—"

"I have a question." One student leaned forward. "Where did you study music, Doctor?"

"St. Petersburg Conservatory in Russia, Mr. Gelbart. Why?"

"What do you play, sir?

"Flute."

Another student snickered, but Mr. Gelbart ignored him. "Would you play something for us, Dr. Derevenko? Please?"

Angry words rushed to Nikolai's tongue, but something in Stephen Gelbart's eyes changed his mind. He lifted his flute from its case. "What would you like to hear?"

"Bach."

Nikolai pressed the instrument against his chin, closed his eyes and played Bach's "Partita in A Minor." The Conservatory of Music in Kansas City disappeared as the lilting melody filled the hall and carried him back to St. Petersburg, to the first time he played with the Philharmonic Orchestra. His father beamed and twelve-year-old Nikolai's chest swelled with joy.

Playing the last few notes, he opened his eyes to see his students circled around him. Tears streamed down Mr. Gelbart's cheeks. For several moments, no one spoke.

Nikolai cleared his throat. "Monday we will discuss the turbulent life of Franz Schubert."

"One more question, sir," whispered Mr. Gelbart. "Is it true you're also a surgeon?"

"Class dismissed."

DR. FLORIN MIKLOS

Having spent the early morning assisting midwife Fruma Ya'el in delivering Nettie Weinberg's baby, Florin ached with exhaustion and happiness. After a mere two hours' labor, she gave birth to a nine-pound boy with a full head of black hair and as lusty a cry as the doctor had ever heard. Never had he experienced such joy! The baby's father, George, broke into song, Nettie's laughter filled the room, and Fruma Ya'el danced with the infant in her arms.

Florin pushed open the clinic door and entered his waiting room where Oxana sat behind the desk with the telephone receiver to her ear. When she saw him, she held her hand over the transmitter. "This woman she is speaking so fast I am trouble to understanding."

"Good English practice for you." He took the telephone. "Is that a new blouse?"

Oxana's taut lips relaxed into a smile. "Catherine picks it out. You like?"

"Lovely. White lace suits you. I don't suppose that stubborn husband of yours has changed his mind about my offer to become the doctor he's meant to be."

"He says music is a calling, too." She pointed to her heart. "But I think here he is not truly happy."

"Bah! Blowing into a tube when he could be saving lives. I shan't give up. No indeed, I will not. Meanwhile," he handed her a dollar, "my dear Mrs. Derevenko, if you would go to the corner restaurant and bring back coffee and toast, I will be forever in your debt."

"I will get it for you now." She stood and pointed to the telephone. "You talk to patient now."

"Yes. Yes, indeed. How could I forget?" Following five minutes of

natter through static, Florin answered the woman's frantic questions. "I'll be happy to lance your son's boil, Madam, but you'll have to take your ailing Fluffy elsewhere. We are not a veterinarian."

DR. ELEANOR WHITAKER
TURNBULL

A statuesque woman, Florin estimated to be at least six feet tall, strolled into his treatment room with the confident air of a politician. Taking off her coat, she tossed her porkpie hat onto the examination table. Her taffy-colored hair sleek and center-parted, shone like China silk. "Are you Dr. Miklos?"

He offered his hand, unable to do anything but gaze into her piercing sorrel eyes. "Who else would I be?"

Running her gloved hand over the top of the medicine cabinet, she bent down and peered at the rows of bottles. "Then I'm in the right place."

She went to the table where his instruments were laid out on a tray. Picking up a pair of scissors, she held them up to the light. "I assume you sterilize. I insist on everything being as clean as humanly possible."

"Oh, my dear lady, I'm sorry you've wasted your time. The nurse-receptionist position has already been filled."

Extending her hand, she held her head high. "I am Eleanor Whitaker Turnbull, *MD*. Now shall we commence the interview or have you filled that position as well?"

HEIRLOOM

Lev rushed into the dining room with an armload of books. "I'm sorry I'm late."

Arel frowned. "Where have you been?"

"I went to Vasily's to study." Lev set his books on the table. "He's a year ahead of me, so he gave me his old textbooks."

Havah set the menorah she had just finished polishing next to the stack of books. "Have you had supper? How was school?"

"School was great and Oxana invited me to eat with them."

"Oh dear, you must be starved."

"Not to worry, Auntie mine." Lev playfully pinched Havah's cheek. "Vasily cooked."

"Vasily is younger than you." Arel thumbed through a book. "Shouldn't you be ahead of him?"

Lev's jaw tensed. "I've missed a lot of school."

"And you're proud of this?"

"Arel, please." Havah's stomach kinked into a knot. "Can't you just be happy he went back to school after dropping out?"

"Damn you, Uncle Arel!" Lev seized the book. "Nothing I do pleases you."

In one heart-stopping motion Arel slapped Lev, toppling the menorah to the floor. It broke in two at Havah's feet. The ground listed beneath her. The color drained from Arel's face. Lev held his book to his chest, Arel's handprint bright on his cheek.

Yussel dropped to his knees and searched for the menorah with trembling hands until he found it. His shoulders sagged as he pressed the two pieces against his heart. Sitting on the floor, he rocked to and fro. Tears soaked his beard as he chanted, "'*Gahm kee elekh b'gay*

tzalmavet . . . yea though I walk through the valley of the shadow of death . . .'"

"It's only one branch, Papa." Havah knelt beside him. "Surely it can be fixed."

"Once a limb is severed, can the tree be made whole again?"

JUDGE WILLIAM H. WALLACE

KANSAS CITY JUDGE IN 1908-PROPONENT OF THE KANSAS CITY BLUE LAW

With his elbow on the counter, Arel rested his chin on his hand. He waved his other hand over an official looking document in front of him. "I'm in big trouble, Havah."

"What's that?"

"It's an indictment from His Honor Judge Wallace. I could go to prison."

"What crime did you commit?"

"I've opened my shop on Sunday instead of Saturday."

"And this is a crime?"

"According to him and his Sunday labor law, we're required to observe the Christian Sabbath or pay a penalty. We may open our shops, but if we sell anything we're in violation."

"I don't understand this man. Ulrich and Dr. Florin call themselves Christians and even go to church on Sunday. They are kind and gentle, nothing like that judge." A lump formed in the pit of Havah's stomach. "Arel, you don't suppose . . ."

She envisioned the police smashing the tailor shop window. They beat Arel with their clubs while he pled for mercy. Next, they came after Rachel. "No!"

Havah shook off her grisly daydream and remembered her chance meeting with President Roosevelt at Ellis Island. Imagine, the ruler of the United States taking the time to speak with a Jewish peasant girl

from Moldavia. Such a man would never allow another Kishinev or Odessa to happen in his great country.

She took the indictment and crumpled it in her fist. "Every ass likes to hear himself bray."

SERGEI DEREVENKO

Nikolai carried his father's bags to Vasily's room. "I hope you don't mind sharing a room, Tatko."

"If my grandson doesn't mind sharing with this decrepit old man, I look forward to it."

Setting Sergei's bags on the bed, Nikolai stared at the man he had not heard from, let alone seen, in over a decade. He was as dapper and well-groomed as ever, although his goatee and mustache were whiter than Nikolai remembered. "You're very thin, Tatko. Are you ill?"

"It's age, that's all. After all these years, you can't expect me to look the same."

Something in the waver of the older man's voice said otherwise. Making it clear he did not want to answer any more questions, Sergei opened his violin case. The Stradivarius shone. "Remember my lover?"

"She's as beautiful as ever," said Nikolai.

"Tonight, we'll give your wife and son a concert such as hasn't been heard in years. This shall be our magnificent prelude to Vasily's commencement ceremony."

"Of course, Tatko." Nikolai stared at him. "Whatever you say, as always."

Sergei's smile faded. He picked up his bow and poked Nikolai's chest. "Vasily tells me you've given up medicine. Are you sure it's the right thing?"

"I should think you'd be happy I've given up, as you phrased it, 'wallowing in blood and bile.'"

Before Sergei could reply, Vasily dragged a trunk through the doorway. "This must have everything you own in it, *Dedushkah*."

Sergei put the bow back in the violin case. "It does."

Nikolai raised an eyebrow. "That's a lot to bring just to take back to Russia."

"I'm not going back."

BURIED DEEP

W hat's the matter with you?" Sergei glared at Nikolai. "You've never told Oxana about your own identical twin brother?"

Oxana seethed. "No. Why should he tell me anything? I am only his wife."

"I don't blame him for keeping it a secret." Sergei took a labored breath. "I'm the one at fault. I used to slap him for even mentioning Bodrik's name."

"He was always so competitive. Had to be the best at everything." Protracted memories zipped through Nikolai's mind. The frozen Neva River ran like a ribbon through St. Petersburg. "'Race you to the bridge,' Bodrik yells. Of course, he's in the lead. Suddenly, the dumb *durak* stops and sticks out his foot. Our skates tangle and I trip. His blade sliced through my leg."

"That explains the scar on your leg." Oxana's frown lessened. "The one you told Vasily was from an angry bear."

"My poor Kolyah did look like he'd been mauled by a bear. I worried I would lose him." Sergei winced. "Bodrik escaped with a simple bump on the head."

"What happened to him?" asked Oxana.

Images, long held at bay, flashed through Nikolai's mind. In the middle of taunting and teasing Nikolai about his clumsiness, Bodrik's smile faded and his body went limp. "He died in my arms that same night."

DANIEL KAMINSKY

Havah admired Daniel Kaminsky who, like her, had lost his parents in a pogrom in Warsaw when he was only in his teens. Being a resourceful boy, he earned enough money to pay his way to America by sweeping floors, chopping wood . . . and picking a few pockets. With only the threadbare clothes on his back and the worn shoes on his feet, he hitchhiked from New York to Kansas City. In twenty-five years, he had built a thriving grocery business. The children loved Daniel, for he filled them with penny candy and stories.

He unscrewed the lid to a jar of red and white candy. "You're coming to Rosie's wedding tonight, yes?"

Havah took a peppermint stick. "I wouldn't miss it."

"It's going to be a magnificent affair. You know my Carla and her love of parties. She and her buddy Zelda have been sewing, cooking, and planning for a month. Nothing like weddings in the old country, eh, Havah? In those days, we were lucky if we got a piece of herring and a slice of dry bread."

"Were you really poor, Mr. Kaminsky?" asked Bayla.

"Was I poor?" He handed her a licorice stick and slipped another into Reuven's pocket. "I was so poor I couldn't afford to pay a compliment." The grocer adjusted his skewed *yarmulke* on his thick auburn hair. "And so hungry, *oy*, I was hungry enough to-to eat *ham*."

INTERFACE

The sewing machine whirred as Sammy Weiner guided a trouser leg under the presser foot. All the while he whistled a cheerful tune. Not only had he lessened Arel's workload in time for the Mayer wedding, he had also lightened Arel's mood. He hummed along with the youth.

Sammy stopped and held up the fruit of his labor. "Whatcha think?"

"What do I think?" Taking the trousers from Sammy, Arel inspected the seams. "I'm a *klug mensch,* a smart man, for hiring you."

"All in a day's work at *Gitterman's Fine Tailoring.*" Whistling, Sammy picked up another pair of half-finished trousers and set to stitching. "Mr. Bader was in yesterday. Love the accent. Sounds like you, Chief."

Arel shrugged. He could not deny that he did not speak English as well as his wife. No one would know by hearing Havah for the first time that she had come from Moldavia. "*Nu?* What about Mr. Bader, already?"

"He says, 'I vant you should make for me a pair of pants.' So, I take out my tape measure to measure his inseam. 'How tall are you, Mr. Bader?' '5 feet and 12 inches,' he says. '6 feet,' says I. 'No,' he scowls at me and wags his finger in my face. 'I am 5 feet and 12 inches.'"

"So, what did you say to that?"

"Who am I to argue? The customer's always right."

MR. SMITH

The odors of ammonia and alcohol made the muggy air in the chemistry lab less than breathable. Dust particles floated on sunbeams pouring through the windows. Lev's collar chafed his neck as he counted the minutes on the clock above the blackboard.

Mr. Smith, the chemistry teacher, strolled down the narrow aisles looking every bit as uncomfortable as Lev. Perspiration collected along his receding hairline and stained his suit under his arms. He stopped at each student's chair to hand out report cards and test results.

Lev's heart thumped against his ribs. Mr. Smith had told the class he would give out the results of the final exam on the last day of school. Lev had studied hard for it, but it proved to be more difficult than he anticipated.

"Mr. Gitterman," said Mr. Smith as he handed a grade card to the girl who sat next to Lev. "Could you remain after class?"

After what seemed a fortnight, the bell rang. The shrill sound made the hair dance across the back of Lev's neck. One by one, his classmates filed by his desk, proffering farewells and best wishes.

The teacher's jaw relaxed and he took off his jacket. "Please excuse the shirtsleeves. Feel free to do the same." Sitting at his desk, he gestured to a chair next to it. "Come closer. My voice has had it."

Lev removed his jacket and stiff collar. A slight breeze cooled his back through his wet shirt. Keeping his eyes on his teacher, Lev sat and braced himself for what he might say next.

Mr. Smith handed Lev an envelope. "Open it."

Lifting the flap with quaking hands, Lev slid out his final exam. The red ink blurred across the top of the page.

"I pride myself on giving rough exams." Mr. Smith chuckled. "No one, in all my years of teaching, let alone a student who moved ahead two grade levels in one year, has gotten a perfect score, until now."

LON M. TILLMAN, MD

PHYSICIAN ON STAFF OF WHEATLEY-PROVIDENT HOSPITAL—THE FIRST NEGRO HOSPITAL IN KANSAS CITY, MISSOURI

Lev combed pomade through his frizzled locks. He felt fortunate to have a friend in Officer Tillman, a former barber who understood the frustrations of kinky hair. When he presented Lev with the tin, he shook his head. "Lev, I suspect there's a Negro in your family's closet somewhere along the line."

"I would be honored, sir."

He remembered the night Officer Tillman found him wandering the streets and convinced him to come home with him.

"Heed my word of advice. Go back to high school and get your diploma, Lev." His dark eyes flashed with conviction as he handed Lev a clean nightshirt. "Education, young man. Education is what sets a man or woman apart."

The next morning, he introduced Lev to his son, the doctor. From that day forward, Lev decided not only to go back to school, but to follow in Dr. Tillman's footsteps. If a black man could overcome the odds stacked against him, so could a Jewish *shtetl* boy.

Setting down his comb, Lev picked up the letter on his desk and read it for the fourth time since the mail came.

"Dear Lev, my friend and future colleague,

"I appreciate the invitation to your commencement ceremony but feel it's within both of our best interests if I decline. I trust you

will understand. Nevertheless, I extend my most heartfelt congratulations on your scholarship to medical school, or as you would say, 'Mazel tov.' Pop and I are pleased you didn't let that brilliant mind of yours go to waste.

"*Perhaps one day you and I will work side by side as we discover a cure for the common prejudice.*

"*Sincerely,*

"*Lon M. Tillman, M.D.*"

WORLD TRAVELER

The train, ultimately headed to New York, rumbled into Kansas City's Union Depot. The ground vibrated under Ulrich's feet. He hoisted Rachel's trunk onto his shoulder. "Are you ready for our adventure, *schatzi*?"

"Our little virtuoso's been ready for days." Havah gazed up at him from her wheelchair. "She's so excited, she hardly slept last night."

Wedged behind Havah, Rachel danced her fingers across an imaginary piano. "My heart's in a whirl! Let's go auto-mo-bubbling, Uncle Uri."

Ulrich cast a questioning glance at Havah.

"It's that silly song about Lucille and her Oldsmobile. She and Papa have worn out his Billy Murray record."

Next to Havah's chair, Arel folded his arms across his chest flashing a smile that did not reflect in his eyes. Ulrich squeezed his forearm. "It's not too late to change your mind, Arel. She's your daughter and Europe is thousands of miles from Missouri."

"Don't you forget it, *my* daughter," whispered Arel. Then he raised his voice, "How could I deprive the world of her great talent?"

"You needn't worry." Catherine bent to kiss Havah's cheek and lifted Rachel into her arms. "We'll care for her as if she were our very own."

"No doubt." Arel planted loud kisses on Rachel's nose and forehead. "You be a good girl, Rukhel Shvester, you hear?"

"I will." Rachel threw her arms around his neck. "G'bye, Poppy. G'bye, Mommy."

Havah paled as if she had been dealt a swift blow. Ulrich's heart cratered to his stomach. Aside from her rounded belly, she looked thin and frail. He knelt and took her hands in his. "Are you sure, Havah? Absolutely certain?"

"Three months is a long—Yes, I'm sure."

TWO SPEEDS FORWARD—
ONE REVERSE

Trees whizzed by in a green haze as Vasily drove his Buick along Holmes Street where the pavement ended. His long hair blew straight out behind him. Choking on the dust, Lev shouted over the sputtering motor. "How fast are we going, Ace?"

"Only thirty miles per hour." Vasily winked at Lev. "We can go faster if you want. It'll go up to forty-five."

"No thanks." The front passenger side tire hit a bump and Lev bounced off the seat. His pulse thumped against his temples. "Hey! Keep your eyes on the road!"

"Can you believe *Dedushkah* gave me my own automobile, albeit secondhand, just for graduating high school?"

"Is he okay?" Lev yelled. "He doesn't look well."

Vasily slowed the car and parked it by the side of the road. "Can I level with you?" He slipped off his goggles. "Tatko thinks he's protecting me by not talking to me about it, but I don't need a doctor to tell me my grandfather's days are numbered. He's lost so much weight since he's been here and sleeps almost all the time. Sometimes he even nods off at dinner, in the middle of his own conversation. Yesterday, he forgot who I was and called me Bodrik."

Lev searched for the right words. "I'm sorry, Vasya."

"At least he came to our commencement." Vasily reached over and slapped Lev's shoulder. "And what about you, Dr. Gitterman? Central High's valedictorian with a scholarship to University of Kansas Medical School." Vasily put his palms together and bowed his head over his fingertips. "Your Majesty, I am not worthy."

"Aw, cut it out!"

JOHANNES BRAHMS

PART 1

Ulrich's return to Vienna unexpectedly stirred memories and emotions he had locked away. Sitting at the upright piano the hotel had provided for him and his prodigy, he lost himself in a favorite piece of music. The lively composition held a special place in his heart and never failed to brighten his mood.

Rachel crawled up onto the bench and sat quietly beside him until he had finished. "I like that, Uncle Uri. Will you teach me to play it?"

He took her hands in his. "Perhaps when these fingers grow a bit longer."

She pulled out of his grasp, positioned her hands on the keyboard and played a few bars of the piece he had just performed. "Like that?"

"You are a wonder, my little Beethoven."

"I can't be Beethoven. He was deaf. I'm blind. Did he compose that song?"

"No, my dear. That was 'Hungarian Dance No. 5' by Johannes Brahms."

"One, two, three, four, five." She counted on her fingers. "Did he write four more Hungarian dances?"

"Smarty girl. He actually composed twenty-one, but the fifth shall always be my favorite." Ulrich gathered the child onto his lap and rested his chin on top of her head. "I will never forget the day I played it for him."

JOHANNES BRAHMS

PART 2

I was only a lad, not much older than you, when I met Mr. Brahms, the great composer." Ulrich rose from the piano with Rachel in his arms. He sank into the wingback chair by the window overlooking the hotel's courtyard. The sun warmed his face. "On my eighth birthday, my grandfather presented me with a grand piano and invited all of his wealthy friends to show it off."

"And Mr. Brahms was there?"

"Not at first. In fact, he angered Grandfather with his tardiness. Half of the guests had come and gone by the time the great composer made his entrance. And what an entrance! Long white hair and a shaggy beard to match, dressed like a pauper with a tattered coat that went below his knees. If that wasn't bad enough, he insulted the adults by ignoring them and gave out candy to us children."

"He sounds nice."

"He would've loved you, my dear. Now, where was I? Oh yes, he comes right up to me and says, 'Hello there, young man. If I'm not mistaken, it's your birthday. They wouldn't lie to me, would they?' He sits on the piano bench beside me and says in the most booming voice you've ever heard, 'Now let me judge whether or not your grandparents wasted their ill-gotten gains on this pretentious monstrosity. Play something.'"

"What did you play?"

"What do you think?"

"'Hungarian Dance No. 5?'"

"What else?"

"Were you scared?"

"Terrified. Afterward, everyone applauded except for Herr Brahms. He glares at me with those piercing blue eyes and asks, 'Where did you

find that piece of rubbish?' When I confess that I stole the sheet music from the *Musikverein*, he throws back his scruffy head and laughs so all of Vienna could hear him. Then he places his hand on my head and says these exact words, 'I'm sorry to be the one to tell you. You're destined to become a renowned pianist. May God have mercy on your tender soul.'"

WUNDERKIND

If Ulrich had harbored any misgivings about whisking four-year-old Rachel away from her parents in Kansas City to take her on tour, she dispelled them, concert after concert. Never was he prouder of her than this night as she performed for over two thousand people at the *Musikverein*. Perhaps if she could see them, she might be frightened, but he had his doubts.

After she played "Für Elise" and Mozart's "Turkish March" without missing a note, Ulrich sat her on a cushion beside him.

The conductor of the Vienna Philharmonic, baton in hand, bowed. "Next, *Herr* Dietrich and *Fräulein* Gitterman will perform a particular favorite of mine, Johann Strauss' 'Vienna Waltz Number Four.'"

Once they finished the duet, the audience burst into applause with shouts of "Brava!"

Rachel, holding tight to Ulrich's hand, followed him to center stage where she curtsied and blew a kiss to the audience.

FUROR

Deep satisfaction surged through Ulrich. Four-year-old Rachel enthralled audiences across Europe, from Colston Hall in Bristol to, just days before, Vienna's *Musikverein*.

To celebrate, he decided it was high time to show Catherine around his boyhood home. The steady clop of the horses' hooves along the cobblestones lulled Ulrich as they made their way around the circular courtyard called the *Schwarzenbergplatz*.

In the midst of a large round pool, a geyser-like fountain, spotlighted from below, illuminated the night sky by turns, with purple, blue, yellow, green, and red.

He stopped the carriage. "The famous *Hochstrahlbrunnen* fountain."

Catherine clapped her hands. "It's simply gorgeous!"

A strident voice split through the peaceful water's swooshing. A rail-thin youth gestured with the fervor of one addressing thousands rather than one equally scrawny youngster.

"These strange ones with their ugly language that sounds like snuffles and squeaking and their odd dress have no place here. We are Germans. '*Deutschland über alles!*'"

Ulrich's neck prickled with more than summer heat as he approached the two young men. Clicking his heels, he bowed and offered his hand. "*Guten abend. Ich bin Ulrich Dietrich.*"

"Oh, *ja.*" The darker-haired of the two boys stiffened and stepped back. "The pianist with his blind *Juden* spawn."

Grateful Rachel did not understand German, Ulrich glowered. "What do you mean *Juden* spawn, sir?"

"You're an educated German—"

"Austrian."

"—and a celebrated musician. Surely, you've read Wagner's *Jewishness in Music* or Treitchske's historic essays. Clearly the Jews are a lesser species."

ZWEI JUNGENDLICHE

Ulrich's hands trembled as he threw off the covers and pushed back his hair, drenched with sweat.

Beside him, Catherine sat up. "Can't you sleep either, dearest? This Vienna heat's dreadful, isn't it?"

He swung his legs over the side of the bed and padded to the hotel window. "I wish it were just the heat, *liebling*."

Staring out at the city of his childhood, he pressed his forehead against the glass. He tried to concentrate on the architecture that had fascinated him as a boy. No matter what he did he could not block the image of the young men at the *Hochstrahlbrunnen* fountain.

The fairer youth, who introduced himself as August Kubizek, seemed cordial enough and even complimented Rachel's talent. However, Ulrich would never forget the way his friend sneered at her as if she were an insect.

"Did you notice his eyes, Cate?"

"They were very blue, weren't they?"

"Sinister. There's something evil about him."

"That skinny little boy? What harm could he do?"

"Just the same, I'll remember his name, Adolf Hitler."

WINONA MINKOWSKI

With a brightly colored shawl covering her head, Winnie lit the candles and circled her hands around them three times to usher in the Sabbath. Pressing her fingertips against her eyelids, she uttered the same blessing the women in Lev's family had recited every Friday night since he could remember, yet it did not sound the same.

Keeping her eyes shut, Winnie picked up a wooden hoop with rawhide stretched over it and a leather mallet. "Now, I'll sing it the way my mother taught me in her Algonquin language."

The rhythm of the drumbeat, coupled with Winnie's mystical intonation and lilting voice, sent pleasurable shivers through him.

She opened her eyes and smiled, teeth shining like polished seashells. *"Gut Shabbes.* Will you say the prayers over the wine and the bread, Lev? My ears have itched to hear a man recite them since Pa died." Taking a *yarmulke* from her pocket, she fondled it between her fingers. "This belonged to him. Let me put it on you."

Her blue calico dress accentuated the violet of her eyes and bronze skin. Cinched at the waist, it revealed her curves, unhampered by a corset. The fragrance of summer blossoms emanated from her as she placed the skull cap on his head. Even with her short black hair and coveralls when they first met, how could he have ever mistaken her for a boy?

His hand trembled as he raised the wine glass and sang, *"Barukh asah, Adonai Eloheynu, Melekh HaOlam* . . . Blessed are You, Oh Lord our God, ruler of the world . . ." He caught a glimpse of Winnie, her eyes trained on him. With a dry cough, he swallowed and continued. *". . . boray p'ree, . . .* who created the fruit . . ." Sweat trickled down the side of his face and dripped between his neck and shoulder top. *". . . ha gahfen . . .* of the vine. Amen." He took a sip of wine and offered her the cup.

Her delicate mouth hugged the rim as she drank. When she gave it back to him, she held his hand in both of hers and leaned into him, her warm breath on his face.

His lips grazed hers ever so slightly. "Winnie?"

"Yes, Red Bird?"

"I'm . . . I'm glad you're not a boy."

VOCATION

His own words to the expectant father, *'Thirty percent chance of survival'* whirled through Nikolai's mind as he approached the operating table, holding his scrubbed hands aloft.

"Welcome back to surgery." Florin's piercing eyes grilled him. "Are you quite ready, Dr. Derevenko?"

The back of his neck prickled. Taking a scalpel from the tray of instruments to his right, his lips quivered in an attempt to mirror the other doctor's reassuring smile. "As ready as a first-year medical student, Dr. Miklos."

"I've every confidence in you, Dr. Derevenko."

Nikolai poised the scalpel over the unconscious mother's abdomen. "That's one of us, Dr. Miklos."

With one deft stroke, Nikolai sliced through layers of skin, while Florin recounted his actions to the audience. "Dr. Derevenko has made a transverse incision in the lower segment of the uterus."

Nikolai's mind flashed to the carnage in Kishinev and Odessa. Children savagely torn apart. Pregnant women gutted. He shook his head and blinked, desperate to concentrate on the present.

Using surgical scissors, he cut through fat, subcutaneous tissue, and into the womb. Reaching into the incised uterus, he found the baby's head. Flexing it from side to side, he worked to slide the child closer to the opening. All the while, Florin intoned his every move to the students.

After two long minutes, Nikolai managed to inch the baby's head out into the open and unwrapped the cord from its neck. With a few gentle tugs, he pulled the baby from the womb. The infant let out a lusty squall.

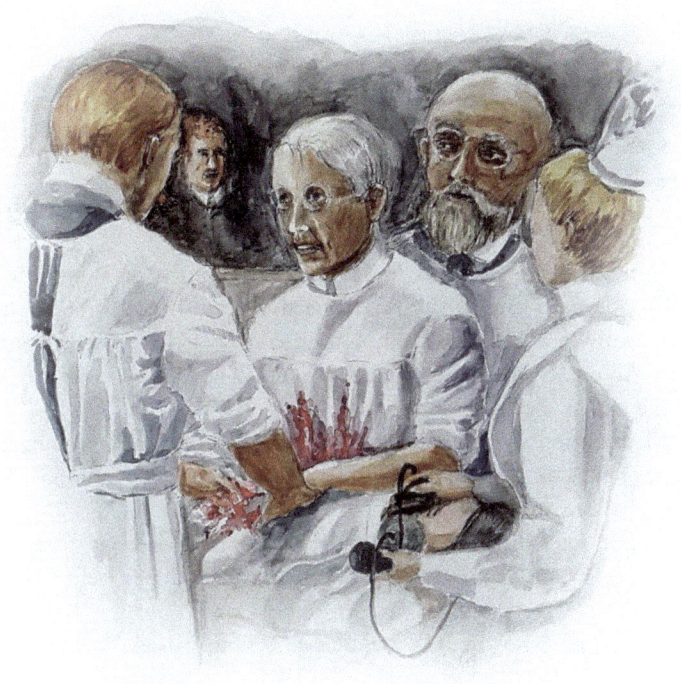

The nurse held her stethoscope's bell against the patient's chest. "Her heartbeat's erratic, Doctor."

"Blood pressure?"

"Dropping."

"Come on, my little Spartanette. We've seen too much together," Nikolai whispered. "Don't give up on me now."

EIGHTH DAY

Arel sat beside the low table, his *tallis* draped over his shoulders and his *tefillin* strapped about his head and arm. Yussel stood behind him, ready to conduct the commandment of *Bris Milah,* the circumcision. An empty chair, left for the prophet Elijah, sat on the other side of the table.

Tears stung Arel's eyes. A week ago, the doctors offered him little hope of his wife and child surviving the birth. He struggled to say, "The Almighty has smiled on me at last."

"*Kvell* later, little brother." A trickle escaping his own eye, Itzak adjusted his *tefillin* and *tallis.* "Let's get the kid clipped before his bar mitzvah."

"May he who cometh be blessed," sang Yussel, heralding the *kvateren.*

Traditionally the *kvateren* would be the godparents, but Arel and Havah agreed the honor of bringing the baby should be given to his older brothers. Lev and Reuven, with proud smiles, entered the room carrying him on a pillow between them.

Yussel continued to chant the blessings. "Happy is he whom Thou choosest and bringeth nigh that he may dwell in Thy courts."

Lev laid the baby, pillow and all, on the table. Arel poured a drop of wine into the baby's mouth.

"Hashem's presence has been waiting," said Yussel, "to bring this child, this son of Israel, into the holy covenant of circumcision."

NAMESAKE

Following his circumcision, Havah cradled her newborn, swaddled in Arel's prayer shawl, in her arms. "My miracle son."

He stretched and yawned. Rachel grazed her fingers over his nose. "Can my baby brother see, Mommy?"

Havah had asked herself the same question. In the past eight days, the baby had hardly opened his eyes. As though he understood his sister, he opened his dark eyes and squinted at the sunlight streaming through the window.

Havah heaved a sigh of relief. "Yes, Rukhel Shvester, your baby brother can see."

"Does he have a name?"

Yussel turned his face toward Havah. "The honor belongs to his mother. *Nu*, Haveleh? This ceremony cannot end until the child has been named."

Havah bundled the baby against her chest and studied the group gathered around her. Among them, Nikolai stood arms over shoulders between Florin and Ulrich. She could not remember seeing such serenity on his face. "I owe you my life, Dr. Nikolai."

He pursed his lips and gave his head a slight shake. "No, Havah, I owe you mine."

She drew a deep breath and exhaled slowly. "His Hebrew name shall be known in the House of Israel as Shimon, for my father, Shimon Cohen, of blessed memory. And he shall be known in Kansas City as Simon Nikolai Gitterman."

CODA

"Mama, Rachel won't stop talking. I can't sleep."

"Bayla's hogging the whole bed."

Reuven chimed in. "They're both noisy, Mama. I can't concentrate on my book."

In the midst of the bickering, Simon's whimpers turned to wails. Havah headed her chair toward the boys' room. "He can't be hungry, I just fed him."

"Mama! Simon went stinky."

"You relax." Arel steered her to the piano. "I'll change his diaper."

Havah positioned her fingers on the piano keys.

"Middle C is where it all begins," said Ulrich when he first taught her to play.

She would never forget the day Ulrich introduced her to the music of Frederic Chopin. He poised his hands over the keys. "He was one of the world's greatest composers. Close your eyes and see where it takes you."

From the first resounding chords of "Nocturne in C-sharp Minor" a flood of emotion coursed through Havah like a river current. In a moment, she was both callow child, alive with anticipation, and wizened matron, bone weary and full of years. Her mother's voice lulled and comforted her with a song about raisins and almonds. Her father's face glowed by candle flame as he poured over volume after volume of Talmud.

As she played the ending notes, her parents vanished, leaving her alone in her living room. Tree shadows danced across the floral wallpaper in the moonlight. Sweet exhaustion engulfed her.

Behind her Arel whispered, his breath warm in her ear. "May I escort you to bed, m'lady?"

She melted into his embrace. "How long have you been there?"

"Long enough to enjoy the concert."

AUTHOR'S NOTE

Dear Reader,

Thank you for reading *A Stone for the Journey*, the companion to the Havah Gitterman Trilogy. It's our hope that you will read the novels to fill in the 'blanks' left by this collection. Havah has so much more story to tell.

On a final note, reviews are so important. A kind word on Goodreads, B&N, and Amazon would be much appreciated by this author.

Shalom,
Rochelle

GLOSSARY

YIDDISH WORDS

A Shaynem Dank: Thank you very much.

Adoshem: A combination of the Hebrew words *Adonai*—Lord and *HaShem*—The Name used by the very Orthodox as a term of respect for the Father.

Azay gezundt: Live and be well.

Bris: Rite of circumcision when a baby boy is eight days old.

Bubbe: Grandmother.

Cholent: A stew made on Friday and kept warm for lunch on the Sabbath. This way no work, such as cooking, is done.

Dibbyk: Demon.

Feh!: Exclamation of disgust or disapproval.

Feygeleh: Sissy, little birdie.

Fraylin: Formal way to address an unmarried woman, i.e., Miss.

Froi: Formal way to address a married woman, i.e. Mrs.

Gut Shabbes: Good Sabbath.

Heder: (literally "a room" in Hebrew) An elementary school where Jewish boys were taught religion and Hebrew. Usually, it was one room.

Humash: First five books of the Bible. The Torah in printed form.

Hupah: Marriage Canopy.

Kasha: Buckwheat Cereal.

Kesubah: Marriage contract.

Kugel: A casserole made with noodles and eggs.

Mensch: A person; usually a good person.

Mitzvah: A good deed.

Nu?: So?

Punim: Face.

Reb: Address for a man, i.e. Mr.

Shabbes: Sabbath.

Schlemiel: A fool.

Shadkhan: Matchmaker.

Shah!: Silence!

Shokhet: A person trained and certified by the rabbi to butcher animals and birds according to Jewish dietary laws.

Shiksah: A non-Jewish woman; usually used in a derogatory manner.

Shmata: A rag.

Shul: How the Orthodox refer to the synagogue.

Shtetl: A Jewish village.

Tsimmes: A dish made with raisins, sweet potatoes, carrots and honey.

Vontz: Bedbug.

Yenta: A gossip, busybody.

Zaydeh: Grandfather.

RUSSIAN WORDS

Dedushkah: Grandfather.

Lapochka: Little sweetie.

Pogrom: An organized massacre against helpless people, particularly the Jews.

Solnyshko: Term of endearment meaning "little sun." Nikolai has called Vasily this since his infancy and refuses to stop even into his son's adolescence.

Tatko: A Slavic word for Papa. Not exactly Russian, but it's what Nikolai calls his father and Vasily calls Nikolai.

Zaychik: Term of endearment meaning "bunny."

Zdrastuyteh: Hello (very formal).

Zjid or *Zhid*: Pejorative Russian term for Jew.

GERMAN WORDS

Liebling: Sweetheart.

Schatzi: Ulrich's favorite term of endearment for Rachel.

Zwei Jungendliches: Two Youths.

ACKNOWLEDGMENTS

Twelve years ago, the desire came to tell the lesser known stories of the pogroms in Eastern Europe with a sense of urgency. These massacres of Jewish people, sanctioned by the Russian government, are the reason my grandparents came to the United States from Poland, Russia, and Lithuania. Their determination, to forge new lives as American citizens, formed Havah's journey.

Countless people have helped me along the path from that first very rough draft to publication and I want to take some time to thank them.

First and most important, thanks to my husband Jan Wayne Fields who has waited on late dinners while "loving" me alone to write. He's my roadie and the loudest voice hawking my wares at book signings and art fairs. Without his dedication, none of this would be possible. Thank you, m'luv.

A special thank you to Jean L. Hays for all of her critiques. Just as writers thrive on constructive criticism, an artist needs a keen eye to see those little things that are out of proportion or perspective. Thanks, Taffy. No doubt Mrs. Spears is smiling down on us, feeling pleased with herself for introducing us 'all those years ago.'

To my friend in the forest, Douglas M. MacIlroy. Thank you for your keen eye when it comes to the technical things, thus saving me from embarrassment. The bell clangs for thee.

To the memory of the crusty old cowboy, Dusty Richards, who didn't spare my feelings, but pointed me in the 'write' direction.

Everyone has that certain friend known as her BFF. Mine is Regina O'Hare who will always be hunky dory in my book.

To Barbara Sherwin who shares similar family stories and memories. So glad we found each other, *Kvetch*.

Many thanks and shalom to Bruce McClain, an artist in the highest degree, for helping me to discover my authentic self.

To Kent Bonham, my cousin and partner in crime.

Todah Rabbah to my *rebbe*, Shmuel Wolkenfeld for my late-in-life Jewish upbringing.

To Lois Hounshell who's listened to every draft and rendition of everything I've written over the past twelve years. Thank you.

Thank you to Susan Hawes who encouraged me to tell my stories and gave Pavel Trubachov his mission statement.

Thanks to Dale Rogerson for her encouragement, friendship, and being the president of my fan club (if I had a fan club). I hope one day to meet you in the flesh. Meanwhile, I'm grateful for the social media that has thrown us together.

A special shout out goes to the "The Dinner Writers": Annette Williams, Polly Swafford, Julie Harris, Annie Withers, and Pat Clothier, of blessed memory. These seasoned writers took me under their collective wings and urged me upward.

Thank you to Danny Maseng, an amazing poet, rabbi, singer, and storyteller for his permission to use his poem, the inspiration for my title.

To my agent, Jeanie Loiacono. This book is the result of your belief in me as a visual artist as well as your support of me as an author. *Danke schön.*

Thanks to William Connor who decided that publishing a coffee table book was a good idea.

ABOUT THE AUTHOR

Rochelle Wisoff-Fields is an author and illustrator. A woman of Jewish descent and the granddaughter of Eastern European immigrants, she has a personal connection to Jewish history, a recurring theme throughout much of her writing. Heavily influenced by the Sholem Aleichem stories, as well as *Fiddler on the Roof,* her novels *Please Say Kaddish for Me, From Silt and Ashes,* and *As One Must One Can* were born of her desire to share the darker side of these beloved tales.

A Kansas City native, Wisoff-Fields attended the Kansas City Art Institute, where she studied painting and lithography. She maintains her blog, *Addicted to Purple,* and is the author of *This, That and Sometimes the Other,* an anthology of her short stories, which she also illustrated. Her stories have also been featured in several other anthologies, including two editions of *Voices.* Wisoff-Fields and her husband, Jan, have three sons and now live in Belton, Missouri.

ROCHELLE WISOFF-FIELDS

FROM OPEN ROAD MEDIA

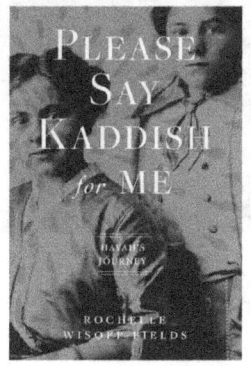

OPEN ROAD

INTEGRATED MEDIA

OPEN ROAD

INTEGRATED MEDIA

Find a full list of our authors and
titles at www.openroadmedia.com

FOLLOW US
@OpenRoadMedia